DANTE

DI SALVO CRIME FAMILY

BOOK TWO

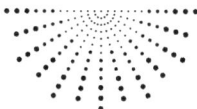

CAMERON HART

WANT A FREE BOOK?

Sign up for my newsletter and get your copy of Chasing Stacy.

River: One look at the stunning waitress carrying the weight of the world on her shoulders, and I'm a gonner. I wasn't looking for a sweet little thing with auburn hair and more baggage than I can fit on the back of my bike, but there's no going back now. She's mine. I'll prove to her I'm more than capable of handling her past and making her feel safe again.

CONNECT WITH ME!

Check out my website, cameronhart.net, for sneak previews on my latest projects.

Follow me on social media:
- Facebook Page
- Facebook Group
- TikTok
- Instagram
- Goodreads
- Bookbub

DANTE

I haven't seen my old man in years, and I like it that way. Being the second in command of the Di Salvo crime family has kept me plenty busy, not to mention paid for my father's expensive in-home care after he spent his life searching for happiness in the bottom of a bottle.

With the threat of war looming overhead, I don't have time to worry about my father's latest health scare. Until I hear her voice. Cambria.

We've texted in the few months she's been working as my father's nurse, but we've never actually spoken. She tells me it's time for me to come visit before it's too late.

I try brushing her off, but somehow, I find myself on a private jet, heading back home. I wasn't sure what to expect, but it certainly wasn't the stunning, too sweet, too tempting Cambria. She doesn't belong in my world, but I can't stay away.

When my woman becomes a pawn in a much bigger and more dangerous game, I jump into action. I'm going to get my girl back, and then I'm going to do whatever it takes to keep her forever.

CHAPTER ONE

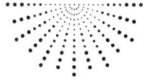

DANTE

*R*omeo leans back in his dark brown leather chair, folding his arms over his chest as he looks around the room at his most trusted men. As the second in command of the Di Salvo crime family, I sit on Romeo's right side during these meetings as a symbol of respect and power. Next to me is Armando, the meat-headed Enforcer, and across from me is Valentino, one of our top Capos.

"After the incident last month, we've beefed up security," Romeo states.

Heads nod around the room, everyone remembering when Romeo's woman, Thalia, was lured away and taken by our rivals, the Colombo family.

The Don goes on to detail the changes around the compound as well as safety precautions for when Thalia goes outside. I try to pay attention, but my goddamn phone has been vibrating in my pocket for the last twenty minutes.

I know who it is without looking. Cambria, my father's nurse. I also know what the text says without even reading it. She wants me to go to Chicago and visit my old man.

Not a fucking chance, sunshine.

I pay for the very best in-home healthcare, the most up-to-date medical technologies, and the top doctors in the area for my father. Isn't that enough? It's not like I'm taking care of him out of love or gratitude for the cold bastard. He chose to deal with life's blows by falling into a bottle of whiskey and not surfacing until he was diagnosed with kidney disease.

No, I don't do it for that bitter, ugly old man. I do it for my mother, may she rest in eternal peace.

A familiar dull ache forms in my chest, and I rub my hand over my heart to break up the tension. I'm a few years shy of forty, and my mother has been gone for most of them. Still, her death is the one weak spot in my otherwise impenetrable walls. The less I interact with my father, the less I have to think about such sad, troubling things.

My phone buzzes again, and Armando shoots me a glare. I don't acknowledge him, which is a general rule of thumb when dealing with the brute. He would rather storm onto a scene and crack skulls without a second thought. On the other hand, I prefer to lay out all of our options, study the eventual end of each of them, and then choose the wisest path accordingly. Needless to say, we don't see eye to eye on much, but Romeo has reminded me over and over not to question who he brings into the inner circle. At the end of the day, I trust Romeo more than I dislike Armando, so it is what it is.

Sliding my phone out of my pocket, I unlock it and stare at the thread of texts from Cambria.

Cambria: *Morning, Mr. Santarossa! Just checking to see if you have any time this week to come to see your father?*

Cambria: *I know you're a busy man, but surely you can spare a few days for family.*

Cambria: *I think you'll be impressed with the progress we've made despite the setbacks this year.*

I don't ask what the setbacks were. I don't care. I pay Cambria and the company she works for a handsome sum to deal with the ups and downs of caring for a cranky old man. Besides, he hasn't kicked the bucket yet. He'll probably outlive us all, fueled only by bitterness and hate.

Cambria: *Yoga has helped with some of the muscle and joint stiffness, and believe it or not, I got your father hooked on meditating in the mornings!*

My eyes roll to the back of my head at the mention of yoga and meditation. If Cambria weren't the best nurse we've had to date, I'd tell her exactly what I think about all that new-age bullshit.

As it is, she's lasted three times as long as any of the previous nurses. Between my father's grumpy ass and my supposedly *unrealistic standards*, the two of us have managed to run off everyone who has applied for that job within a few months. Sometimes a few weeks. One lady quit on her first day.

But Cambria has been with my old man for over a year, so that counts for something. It certainly says a lot about her constitution. From personal experience, I know it's hard to please my dad, and according to the dozen or so nurses who came before, I'm just as impossible to deal with.

Personally, I think the younger generation isn't used to hard work. They want to be coddled, but that's not how the real world works. I don't have time to hold the hand of every caregiver who dares to take up the challenge that is Raul Santarossa, so having Cambria be so competent was a much-needed breath of fresh air.

Until she started in on this whole coming-for-a-visit thing. That shit is getting old real quick.

I stare at the screen, watching those three little dots bounce up and down, indicating she's working on another text. She's persistent, I'll give her that much.

Cambria: *Maybe you could try meditating when you're here. It's a total game-changer!*

For some reason, this is what triggers me to respond. My fingers start typing before my brain has a chance to catch up.

Dante: *I have never, and will never, meditate.*

Cambria: *Raul said the exact same thing!*

I growl at her response, then shove my phone in my pocket again. Romeo turns his attention toward me, giving me a hard glare. I straighten up and nod once, letting him know I'm here and I'm all in. No more distractions.

My phone buzzes again, but I remain resolute, focusing on Romeo's update about the Colombos and our deal with the meat packing plant union. Everything got fucked up last month when the Colombos tried moving in on our territory and taking over our money-laundering operation via the union pension funds. Shit hit the fan, and our contact was shot in the head, along with his goon, who just so happened to be Thalia's brother.

A new head of the UFCW union has been appointed, Brent Carmichael. Valentino is working with him to strike up a similar deal to the one we had with his predecessor. It's all good and necessary information, but my mind keeps wandering back to Cambria and her insistence on me seeing my father.

She's been working for me for nearly a year and a half, but only in the last two months has she started on the father/son reunion kick. Why now? Does my old man want to see me? I'm guessing not since he's not the one texting me. How awkward would it be to show up and have my father kick me out? Once was enough for me, thank you.

"Dante," Romeo says, bringing me back to the present moment.

I blink a few times, suddenly aware that everyone else has exited the room.

4

"Yes, boss," I answer, standing to meet him face to face.

"Where were you today?"

"I got up at six, my normal time, and made a breakfast of eggs and toast. Then I did some work from my home office before hitting the gym. I had that lunch meeting in Manhattan, then–"

"Not literally," Romeo grunts, cutting me off.

I furrow my brow, wondering what else he could mean. He asked where I was, and I listed the places I'd been.

"What I mean," Romeo continues, "is that your head was somewhere else during our meeting. What has you so distracted? It's not like you, Dante."

Sighing, my shoulders drop slightly as I think of what to tell the Boss. My phone buzzes again, and Romeo gives me a pointed look.

"Go ahead," he says with a nod. "Answer it. Then tell me who it is and why they have more of your attention than I do."

Swallowing thickly, I pull out my phone and glance at the two texts she sent. Then I take time to really look at them, each word sinking into my stomach like a lead weight.

Cambria: *Your father would kill me for telling you this, but he's had several strokes in the last few months. He likes to think he's invincible, and part of me wonders if you think that, too.*

Cambria: *I don't know anything about your relationship, only that it's obviously complicated. I just feel like you need to know the stakes. Raul's health has taken a turn, and I know you don't want to deal with that, but here we are. Please, please consider visiting your father before it's too late.*

"Well?" Romeo asks.

Taking a deep breath, I decide to get it all out there and ask for his advice. I consider Romeo my closest friend, though I'd never tell him that. Neither of us talks about it, but we both know. That's enough for me.

"My father has been ill for quite some time," I start. Romeo nods, encouraging me to continue. "He's back in Chicago being taken care of by the best of the best. But I guess things have… escalated recently. The nurse thinks I should come for a visit."

"Ah, the nurse who does yoga and meditation?"

I roll my eyes. "Yes."

My friend gets a knowing look in his eyes, though I have no idea about what. It's gone before I can decipher it.

"You should go."

My eyebrows shoot up my forehead, and I blink a few times, wondering if Romeo is kidding. The Don never jokes, though, so he must be… serious?

"I… I can't," I stutter. "What about everything I need to do here? Things with the UFCW union are heating up, not to mention the retribution we're sure to get from the Colombos. I can't leave now."

Romeo studies me carefully for a few moments, then clears his throat. "Dante, I'm temporarily relieving you of your duties to the Di Salvo family."

"What? No, I–"

Romeo holds his hand out, palm up, cutting me off.

"*Temporarily*," he emphasizes. "Just long enough for you to fly to Chicago, see your father, and come back."

"What about the–"

"Colombos won't strike back so soon. They need time to regroup, recover, and replan. In the meantime, I have my Capos working on gathering intel."

"And the union–"

"Will be overseen by myself and Valentino. We will keep you in the loop, of course, but you need not be here."

I press my lips together, trying to think of another excuse, but Romeo has me dead to rights. Anything I come up with, he'll counter.

Nodding in defeat, I reluctantly and morosely agree to take the week off to see my father. Romeo dismisses me, and I step out of his office, pausing to lean against the wall outside.

"Fuck," I mutter under my breath. This is the last thing I want to deal with right now, or ever, for that matter.

Reaching into my pocket, I pull out my phone and start typing a text to the persistent and ever-bubbly Cambria. I'm in the middle of delivering the happy news of my arrival when I receive an incoming call from the woman herself.

I stare at the screen in shock, not sure what to do. She's never called before, only texted or emailed. That's my preferred method of communication, and she knows that. However, what little I know about Cambria tells me that she won't stop at one phone call, so I answer it, bracing myself for what's next.

"Mr. Santarossa?" comes the sweetest voice I've ever heard.

I pull the phone away from my ear and double-check that it's the nurse calling. Indeed, it is Cambria Clayton.

"I know you don't like phone calls, but I felt this was important and wanted to speak with you so the meaning doesn't get lost over text."

I blink a few times, trying to figure out why the hell I'm light-headed and tense at the sound of her voice. It does something to me. Something wholly unfamiliar and unsettling.

"I can hear you breathing, you know," Cambria says. "If you don't want to talk, that's fine. I have a feeling I have enough words for both of us."

I snort at that but cover it up with a cough. This woman shouldn't have the ability to make me laugh. Preposterous.

"I know, I know," she continues. "I'm chatty and enthusiastic about pretty much everything, which isn't everyone's cup of tea. But that's not the point."

I grunt at the idea of someone not liking Cambria and then berate myself for giving a fuck. I don't. I can't.

"The point is, your father might not ever say this, but he misses you. In his own way."

This pulls a dark laugh from the pit of my black soul. "The only thing that man misses is having a handle of whiskey permanently attached to his right hand."

"He speaks!" Cambria exclaims. I'd yell at her for disrespecting me, but she's so genuine in her excitement that I don't have it in me to bring her down a peg. Which isn't like me. Not at all.

"You'll be pleased to know I will be in Chicago this week. I'll catch the first flight out in the morning."

"You are correct," Cambria answers, her voice in a lower pitch, presumably in an attempt to match mine. "I am *very* pleased."

What other ways could I pleasure you?

Jesus fuck, where did that come from? Not only is it inappropriate, but I can't remember the last time someone elicited that kind of response from me. I can honestly say I've never reacted to anyone like this, let alone someone I haven't even officially met.

"Good," I manage to choke out. "I'll be there mid-morning tomorrow."

"Thank you, Mr. Santarossa! You won't regret–"

I hang up before she can finish that sentence. Her melodic voice and boisterous laughter are messing with my head. Besides, she's wrong. I'm sure I'll have nothing but regret after visiting my father, but I view this as another mission from Romeo. He told me to deal with my dad and return ready to fight.

That's precisely what I'm going to do. Nothing more.

CHAPTER TWO

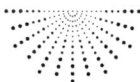

CAMBRIA

"All right, Mr. S, it's about time to get ready for bed," I tell my client, Raul Santarossa.

He narrows his eyes at me. "One more game." His voice is gravelly, worn by decades of drinking and smoking, from what I've gathered.

"That's what you said last time," I point out, raising an eyebrow at the old man.

He tries his hardest to scowl, but a smile is buried deep down there somewhere. He even lets me see it sometimes.

"But fine, one more. Then you get ready for bed while I get your meds."

A spark of triumph lights up Raul's brown eyes, making him look like a mischievous little kid as he gathers the Connect Four pieces and separates them into colors. How can anyone not find him adorable?

When I first took the job, Raul was a little rough around the edges. We had some hard days where he was a stubborn jerk, but I showed him I'm equally as stubborn when it comes to taking care of people. It's my job as an in-home nurse and caregiver, and truly an act of love for each of my clients.

I know all too well what it's like having gruff, jaded healthcare workers mishandling the most important person in my life. I want to make sure I treat everyone with the kindness and grace I wish had been afforded to my mother.

"Ready?" I ask, pushing away the painful memories of those last few months of her life.

"Born ready," Raul replies, his eyes focused on the slotted game board positioned between us.

I smile at his seriousness over a simple children's game. The second week I worked for the Santarossas, I picked up a few board and card games from a local thrift shop and brought them over. I wasn't sure if Raul would go for it, and for a while, he didn't. The games sat in the corner of the living room, unopened.

Then one morning, I arrived early and set up the Connect Four game on the kitchen table, along with a deck of Uno cards. Raul wanted nothing to do with the cards, but he quickly became fascinated with the strategy behind Connect Four. We played a few rounds that morning, and he tried to act disinterested. However, when I moved to put it away, he stopped me and asked for one more game.

Now, we play Connect Four almost every evening before bed.

I drop one of my red chips into a slot on the board and watch in amusement as Raul furrows his brow. He glances at his black chips, then back to the rows and columns on the board.

Everyone at the in-home nursing agency I work for warned me away from taking the Santarossa job, saying the old man's bad attitude was only rivaled by his son's. After one conversation with Raul, I knew he was a softie at heart.

He has a prickly exterior to scare people off and a lot of shame about his past that keeps him isolated.

He just needed someone to be kind and patient and give him the benefit of the doubt. Raul also needed someone to stand up to him and let him know when he was being an asshole. So far, I've managed the perfect balance of each.

I wish those tactics worked on his son.

Dropping another red chip onto the board, I laugh when Raul curses under his breath.

I may have cracked the code on Mr. Santarossa, but Dante is a different story. He's gruff like his father but more detached. Very professional, yet cold and stiff. Stuck-up. A smirk spreads across my face as I remember his response to trying meditation.

I have never, and will never, meditate.

Speaking of Dante, it's probably time I tell Raul about his visit. Truthfully, I wasn't expecting Dante to give in. I've been needling him about coming to Chicago for weeks, if not months. Now that he's booking a flight and headed this way, I need to figure out how to break the news to Raul.

I put my last red chip into one of the remaining slots and watch Raul grin from ear to ear as he plays his last chip, getting a connect four. This is as good a time as any since this is the only time he allows himself to feel happiness.

"I've got some good news," I start, plastering on an enthusiastic smile.

"Is it that I won for the fifth time in a row?" he gloats.

I roll my eyes and start to put the game away. "It's about your son."

Raul drops the chips he's holding and blinks a few times before looking up at me.

I'm on a roll now, so I keep going. "He's coming for a visit. Isn't that great?"

Dark brown eyes fix on mine, and while he's trying to be angry, I see his true emotion. Fear.

"Why?"

"To see you, of course," I answer lightly.

Raul snorts. "When?"

"Tomorrow."

"What the fuck? When were you going to tell me?"

"Right now," I say firmly, letting him know I won't tolerate his raised voice. "It's a bit last minute, but–"

"A bit? Give an old man time to prepare," he grumbles.

"And what do you have to prepare? Last time I checked, I do the prep work around here."

"Cambria…"

"Mr. S…"

He sighs heavily, resting his head in his hands. "It's complicated between my son and me," he says softly.

I pick up the game and put it away before sitting next to Raul. "I know," I tell him just as softly. "I'm not sure what happened between you two, but don't you think it's time to reconnect?"

"I'm not the only one who hasn't picked up the phone in twenty-five years," he grouses.

"True, but you're the parent. Whether you or your son admit it, you hold a place of power in his life—for better or worse. Don't you want it to be for the better? Lead by example and all that?"

"You don't have a kid. You don't know what it's like when you've fucked up as badly and often as I have."

"That's not fair, and you know it. It's not fair to keep punishing yourself, and it's certainly not fair to your son to let your pride get in the way of having a relationship."

I know I'm being harsh, but I want this reunion to go well. Raul is a tough old man who has weathered a lot in his life, but his health has been fragile for quite some time. The numerous strokes this year took longer and longer to recover from, and this last one cost him quite a bit of mobility. It breaks my heart to think about Raul and Dante not seeing each other at least one last time.

That kind of guilt eats away at your soul, and I wouldn't wish it on my worst enemy—even the cold-hearted, aloof Dante.

I have one last card to play, though I feel bad about bringing it up. Still, I'm doing this for the right reason.

"I know it's hard to talk about, but wouldn't Diane want you and your son to have a relationship?" Bringing up his deceased wife was a low blow, but I know I have him when he dips his head. "You have to try. I'm not saying it will be easy, but nothing worthwhile is."

He nods once, then claps his hands on his knees. "I guess I don't have much of a choice, eh?"

"That's the spirit," I joke, standing and helping him with his walker. "Now go get ready for bed. I'll be in with meds in a few minutes."

Raul waves me off before shuffling down the hall.

I let out a breath and deflate against the kitchen counter. The first two hurdles are now over. First, convincing Dante to visit, and second, getting Raul to agree. While he didn't exactly jump for joy, I'll take his defeated acceptance. It's a start.

Twenty minutes later, I'm locking up the back door to the main house and heading to my studio apartment-slash-cottage across the yard. The other nurses complained about that as well. They didn't like the live-in situation that Dante required and didn't understand why they couldn't go home at night.

Walking in the front door, I look around at the little

home I've created. The nurses who managed to work for the Santarossas for a short time told me the cottage was a depressing hole in the wall, and truthfully, it was in pretty bad shape when I moved in. This place looks much more inviting with a good scrub down, some new lights, a few thrift store paintings, and a gorgeous macrame hanging I found in a dumpster. I even hung a beaded curtain to separate the living area from my sleeping area.

I don't mind the simple living conditions. I'm only here in the evenings and don't need much. After my mother passed, I spent the life insurance money on the funeral and medical bills. When that ran out, I sold our home and nearly everything in it to cover the rest.

I started over with nothing and no one, but I got into a good nursing school. Unfortunately, I had to take out a ton of student loans to make ends meet, even working full-time on top of classes. That's a huge reason I took this job. If I stick with it for three years, my debt will be paid off, and I can start looking for a place of my own.

It's a nice thought.

After kicking off my shoes, I beeline to the bathroom and turn the shower on to its hottest setting. Stripping down, I step under the stream and let the warm water ease my tight muscles.

I'd be lying if I said I wasn't anxious about Dante's visit. He's the mysterious benefactor who lives in New York City and has never, not once, been back to see his father. The two haven't spoken in decades, from what little information I could get from the other nurses and Raul himself.

I'm not sure what to expect. Dante is less than thrilled to be pulled away from his busy, successful life, and I get the sense he finds me annoying. It wouldn't be the first time, but with Dante, it feels different. His opinion of me matters, and I don't want to think about why.

Turning the water off, I dry myself with a towel and pull on my sleep shorts and a comfy tank top. I comb through my wet hair and braid it on the side before climbing into bed. Taking a deep breath, I try to calm my nerves and get comfortable. It's going to be a long day of playing peacemaker tomorrow, so I better rest up.

CHAPTER THREE

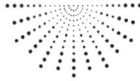

DANTE

I tip the cab driver and gather my shit from the trunk, sighing as I shoulder my bag. Looking at my watch, I groan when I see it's past one in the morning.

I told Cambria I'd be here tomorrow mid-morning, but an earlier flight opened up. I figured the sooner I got here, the sooner I could leave. It seemed like solid logic at the time, but now it's pitch black out, and I don't want to sneak into my old man's house like a thief. Then again, he probably wouldn't expect anything less from me.

Waving the cabbie off, I trudge up the two porch stairs and take a deep breath before opening the door. Only it's locked. Which makes sense. It's the middle of the goddamn night.

Well, this was a stupid idea. What was I thinking? It's not like me to miss an important detail like not announcing my arrival and being locked out. This whole situation has thrown me off my game, and I don't like it. Not one bit.

Looking around the property I bought for my father decades ago, I remember there being a little cottage around back. I'm not sure the last time anyone stayed there, but I've slept in worse places. Besides, it's only for the night. With any luck, I'll upset my father over breakfast and be on my way back to New York before lunch.

I trudge around the side of the house and into the back-yard, frowning when I step in mud.

"Of fucking course," I mutter as I lift my shoe out of the muck. Rationally, I know mud exists in New York City as well. But right now, this is all Chicago's fault.

I eventually find the little structure tucked away in the corner. Finally. I've earned a few hours of shut-eye, however rough they might be.

Gripping the doorknob, I rattle it a few times and shove on the door, stumbling a bit when it gives way. Damn door hardly fits in its frame. I slam it behind me and turn around, only to be assaulted with some sort of net made of beads.

"What the fuck?" I grunt at the same time as a shriek fills the room.

"Stay back!" someone shouts. "I, um, I'm… armed!"

I'd recognize that voice anywhere. As much as I hate to admit it, I heard her voice in my fitful sleep on the plane. I heard it in the cab ride over here. Am I hallucinating it right now?

"Cambria?" I ask as I fight my way out of what appears to be a beaded curtain, not a net.

"No, I'm… Tambria," she says in the most unconvincing voice ever.

"You're a shit liar."

"And you're trespassing."

I manage to untangle myself from the tacky decor, and then I'm face to face with a curvy little ray of sunshine, complete with white-blonde hair that sparkles even in the darkness. Bright blue eyes blink at me, wide and tinged with fear. I'll give her some credit; she may be terrified, but she's standing on her bed, shoulders back, head high, chin out, ready to tackle the monster who woke her. She's clutching something in her right hand, but I don't think it's a gun.

Stupid fucking moron, I berate myself. Of course, the nurse lives here. That's part of her contract. It's not like me to miss these details, and I hate the person I've become, all because of this trip.

Without permission, my eyes wander down the slope of her neck, lower, catching on her generous breasts beneath her barely-there tank top. I can't stop myself from dropping my gaze to her wide hips, my fingers twitching to grab her there and pull her closer, closer, closer until I can feel every single one of her curves pressed against me. Jesus, her thick thighs and shapely calves are on display, those little sleep shorts doing nothing to hide all that skin.

I feel like a feral wolf licking my lips, ready to devour my prey.

"Hey," Cambria spits. "Eyes up here, buddy."

Her forceful tone almost pulls a chuckle out of me. She can't be more than a few inches over five feet, and while Cambria has curves I can't think about, she's petite and no match for me. Still, I respect her spirit, which seems to be about fifteen feet tall.

"I think we got off on the wrong foot," I hedge, stepping toward her with my palms up. I can't say I've ever been in a position of surrender, but something tells me this is the right move. I need a buffer if I want to survive this visit with my dad.

"Yeah, breaking and entering isn't the best first impression," she sasses.

Even though she's encased in shadows, I can see her trembling. Her voice is strong, but it's taking everything for her not to collapse. I can't quite say what that does to me, but I don't think I like her being afraid, and certainly not of me.

"Cambria, I'm not here to hurt you. I'm Dante."

"Dante?" she repeats softly.

Fuck, I like the way she says my name. I like it way too much.

"Dante!" Cambria exclaims, her voice full of warmth and energy.

I don't think anyone has ever been excited to see me, and I'm not sure what to think about it. Everything about this situation is throwing me for a loop.

The curvy little ray of sunshine drops whatever was in her hand, a water bottle, from the looks of it, and hops down off the bed.

"I thought you said you were armed?" I muse, giving the water bottle a pointed look.

"Technically, I *am* armed," she replies, a cheeky grin on her face as she waves her arms in the air.

I can honestly say I'm at a loss for words. Cambria flashes me a bright smile, her light blue eyes sparkling as she grabs a fuzzy robe and wraps it around herself.

She skips into the kitchen area, her braided hair tossed over her shoulder and bouncing behind her.

"I thought you weren't coming until morning," she says over her shoulder as she putters around the kitchen.

I'm frozen in place, watching as this mysterious woman fills up a tea kettle and sets out two mugs, honey, and an assortment of teas.

"Technically, it *is* morning," I answer. Is that my voice? When did it get so deep?

Cambria turns to face me, one hand on her hip as she rolls her eyes. "You know what I mean, smart-ass."

She turns back around and tends to the kettle while I blink a few times and comprehend what the sassy little nurse said to me. She called me a smart-ass. And rolled her eyes at me. No one would dare treat me with such disrespect in New York. If they did, punishment would be swift.

Cambria, however... I want to punish her, too. But my twisted mind and dark, lustful urges don't want to torture her. They want to spank her juicy ass until it's red, then massage her sore skin before starting again, making her count each one.

It takes a moment to realize she's been talking to me. I shake my head at those ridiculous thoughts and try to stay focused. I'm sure it's because I'm tired and out of my element. Nothing more.

"So, yeah. I know there are several empty rooms in the main house, but this works out better for everyone. A little more privacy, but I'm still right here if anything happens. I spruced up the place a little bit when I moved in. Some rugs, a few paintings–"

"Beaded death traps?" I grumble, shooting her a glare.

Cambria smiles and nods. "It worked, didn't it?"

I sigh, wiping a hand down my face. I'm not sure what game we're playing here, but I'm exhausted, and my emotions are all over the place. Strange, because usually, I'm able to shove my feelings down deep and shut the cellar door, never to be heard from again. It's this place. And this woman. Everything will be clearer in the morning.

"Here, it's some sleepy-time tea," Cambria says softly from right beside me.

I startle, not realizing how close she was. "No," I snap, jumping back several steps.

"Relax, I didn't spike it with anything."

"That's not... why would you even say that?"

Cambria shrugs and holds out the drink. "You seem like someone who is always a little suspicious of everyone and everything."

"Well, that's because people and things can't be trusted." I'm not sure why I said that.

Cambria tilts her head slightly, studying me with her

ethereal eyes. I don't like her scrutiny. I'm not sure I measure up, and I can't wrap my head around why I want to.

Finally, she sets the mug on the little breakfast bar in front of me and makes herself a cup of tea. She rests her elbows on the counter, leaning forward slightly as she looks up at me. "Are you going to the main house tonight?"

I find myself shaking my head before I even realize what I'm doing. "I can't," is all I say. I'm not even sure she heard it.

"You're right. It's probably best to get a fresh start in the morning."

I nod, thankful that she doesn't press the issue.

"You finish your tea, and I'll find my sleeping bag. I know I have one around here." Cambria turns to dig through a tiny storage closet behind her. "I'm sure I didn't throw it away," she continues, tossing random things out of the closet as she burrows further inside. "Just in case I need to camp in my car again, you know?"

"You've slept in your car?" I growl, a sudden wave of protectiveness surging through me. It's as confusing as it is fierce.

"Not since getting this job. Thank you, by the way. I never had the chance to thank you in person for hiring me."

I grunt, then tear my eyes away from where the hem of her robe is riding up, giving me a view of those legs and her juicy, round little ass.

"Ah-ha! Gotcha," she says triumphantly. "I'll take the floor, and you take the bed."

A second later, Cambria pulls out a ratty sleeping bag with the liner torn in several places. The thought of her sleeping in her car with that piece of garbage wrapped around her has me feeling some intense emotions I don't recognize.

"You're not sleeping in that," I tell her firmly, walking around the breakfast bar to stand beside her.

"Well, you're certainly not sleeping in it," she counters. "It would barely cover your legs."

"You take the bed, and I'll take the floor. That's final." I reach for the sleeping bag, but Cambria hides it behind her.

"You don't get to barge into my house and make demands, mister." Her blue eyes narrow at me, and goddamn if it's not the most adorable thing I've ever seen. Can't say I've ever used that word to describe anyone before, but it's true.

"You know I'm the one who bought this house, right? And the one who signs your paychecks?"

"Are you trying to bully me, Mr. Santarossa?"

"No, I'm just saying–"

"Let's do rock, paper, scissors for the bed!" Cambria says, cutting me off. "You do know how to play rock, paper, scissors, right?"

"Yes," I say defensively. "Of course."

"Just checking. No offense, but you don't seem the type for schoolyard games."

"What do I seem like?" Why do I keep saying things without thinking them through? It's not like me at all.

Cambria peers up at me, those blue eyes missing nothing as she picks me apart. I feel raw and vulnerable, two things I consider very dangerous.

The curvy goddess smiles softly at me, then shrugs her shoulders. "I guess we'll find out. Now, we're going on three. Ready?" I nod, both of our fists facing off. "One…Two…Three!"

I spread my hand into paper while Cambria keeps her fist balled up for rock.

"Dammit," I curse.

"Yay! You get the bed. It's official."

"Best two out of three?"

"Not a chance," Cambria says with a laugh as she spins away, sleeping bag in hand.

I watch her lay the worn-out piece of shit fabric on the hardwood floor as I take off my shoes, jacket and tie. I packed sweats and a t-shirt, but I don't want to undress in front of her. It feels too personal.

Crawling into the small bed shoved up against the wall, I cover myself with a few blankets and try to get comfortable. All I can think about is Cambria lying on the goddamn ground a few feet away from me. I don't know why I can't let it go. She doesn't care and is willing to give up her bed for the night.

I convince myself everything is fine and it'll only be for the night. Then, for some reason, I open my stupid mouth. "Sleep with me. In the bed. Just sleep. Not… Jesus," I grumble, rubbing my temples.

Cambria giggles, the sound lighter than air. "I'm okay down here."

"I'm not okay with it," I mutter, scooting over in the small bed as far as I can. "Just… just get up here. Don't make it weird."

"If that's not the sweetest invite, I don't know what is," she answers sarcastically.

Despite her sass, Cambria stands, her voluptuous figure silhouetted against the moonlight as she walks toward me. I swear I've had dreams like this.

Before she can see how her presence affects me, I roll onto my side, giving her my back. Jesus, I have to get my raging hard-on under control. Yes, she's undeniably gorgeous and sexy and seductively innocent, but I'm being crazy. It's been a long goddamn day, on top of a long goddamn week, in the midst of a long goddamn month. That's all this is.

The bed dips with Cambria's weight, and she stretches out behind me as she snuggles under the blankets. We're both silent, the cottage filled with just the sound of our combined breaths.

"Want to do a nighttime meditation?" Cambria whispers.

"Hell, no," I grunt.

Cambria giggles again, and dammit, if I don't love every time I can get her to make that sound.

"Just checking. Goodnight, Dante."

"Night, Cambria."

We both lie in the dark stillness, barely touching, as we drift off to sleep. I didn't think I'd be able to get a single wink in, but I already feel more relaxed than I can ever remember. I don't want to think about why.

CHAPTER FOUR

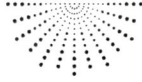

CAMBRIA

*M*y alarm goes off at six-thirty, and I roll over, turning it off without opening my eyes. *Why do I feel like a pile of hot garbage?*

Last night comes back to me in little vignettes. I was startled awake by someone rattling my door and bursting through it. Then a giant beast of a man roared and made an obnoxious commotion, tearing down my beaded curtain like a jerk. I almost squirted him in the eye with my water bottle, but then he introduced himself.

Dante.

God, could he be less perfect? Seriously, it'd be easier to ignore him if he weren't a foot taller than me and rippling with lean muscle beneath his crisp suit. From what I saw of his hands and arms, Dante has tattoos covering his chiseled body. I certainly didn't picture every single place he might have ink on him as I drifted off to sleep last night.

Peering over my shoulder, I'm slightly disappointed to see I'm alone. I'm not sure what I expected. For Dante to wake up and suddenly be a warm and inviting person instead of cold and aloof? I love my sleepy-time tea, but that's a tall order for any beverage.

I climb out of bed and throw on leggings and a sweatshirt before running through my morning yoga stretches. I focus on a posture of open acceptance for whatever the day holds. I have a feeling I'll need all of the mindfulness tools at my disposal to make it through the week.

After stretching, I sit cross-legged on the floor, leaning against the side of my bed. Resting the back of my hands on my knees, I hold my palms open as I silently repeat my intentions for the day; *I release shame, I choose authenticity, and I carry peace within me.*

I'm on my second round of deep breathing when I hear Dante pacing around. Peeking one eye open, my attention is drawn to the kitchen window, where he's stomping in one direction, pausing, spinning on his heel, then stomping in the opposite direction.

"If you need me to come back... No, I haven't seen him yet, but... Yes, Boss. I understand. But you'll still call me if—"

He pulls the phone away from his ear and stares at it. I can't quite see his facial expression from here, but I assume he's trying to melt his phone with laser vision.

"He hung up on me," Dante growls, staring at the cell phone in his hand.

I watch as he shoves it back into his pocket and wipes a hand down his face. Dante's shoulders drop as he lets out a defeated sigh. My heart hurts for whatever weight he's carrying. I don't know what Dante's job is, but I've been told it's very demanding. If he'd let me, I'd give him a shoulder massage and work through a relaxing meditation before showing him some stretches to ease back tension and realign his neck.

As it is, Dante seems to think that if he tried meditating,

he'd burst into flames. That's partially why I'm so determined to get him to do it at least once. The other part of me genuinely believes in the practice of mindfulness, and I think everyone could benefit from a few moments of inner peace.

I close my eyes and get back to my intentions, trying to push thoughts of Dante out of my head. I definitely don't focus on how his taut muscles would feel beneath my hands as I rub the tension from them.

The front door swings open, and in steps Dante. His eyes find mine instantly, and a shiver runs down my spine. I didn't get a good look at his features last night in the dark, but in the cold, hard light of day, I see he's even more handsome than I thought. Damn it.

Deep brown eyes lock onto mine, and I find it impossible to break the connection. He's sharing something with me, but before I can figure it out, he blinks and shakes his head.

"Are you done with your new age nonsense?" he grumbles, waving a hand in my direction.

I smile at the grumpy Dante as he shuts the door and leans against it. "For now," I answer cheerfully, hopping up from the floor. "One of these days, I'll get you to join me. It's not as crazy as you might think."

Dante raises an eyebrow, letting me know he doesn't believe me one bit.

I grab my phone and toss it into my bag, along with a few other things I usually take to the main house.

"Seriously. Most days, it's just stretching and taking a few moments to ground yourself and prepare for the day. Your breath is a powerful tool once you know how to use it. I also paint my face with rabbit's blood and dance naked in the full moon once a month to rejuvenate the crystals I use in my spells, but other than that, it's totally normal."

I wish I could snap a picture of Dante's face right now. It's exactly what I was hoping his reaction would be. His dark eyebrows are hidden somewhere in his hairline, and his eyes are wide as dinner plates as he stares at me. A mixture of disbelief, panic, and what-the-fuck energy pours from him, and I can only hold in my laughter for so long.

"Oh my god, I'm kidding!" I say before breaking down into laughter. Dante's eyes narrow into suspicious little slits, which only makes me laugh harder. "I would never kill a rabbit."

Dante opens his mouth, but I hold my hand up, stopping him. He looks equally as taken aback by that action as he was by my naked moonlight dance, and I won't lie, I love it.

"Kidding again," I tell him with a smile. "I'm not into crystals and don't dance naked, in the moonlight or otherwise."

He mutters something that sounds like, "Too bad."

"What?"

"Nothing."

I stare at him for a moment, trying to figure out what he said. Dante gives nothing away, so I drop it for now.

"It's almost seven, so I need to get up to the main house and start on breakfast and morning meds. Are you ready?"

Dante stares out the window at the main house, a look of unbearable vulnerability cracking his usually rough exterior. I have no idea what happened between him and his father, but I'm having a hard time reconciling the harsh, clipped man from the texts we've shared over the months with the lost man standing in front of me.

He looks so fragile, and I have the urge to hug him. I don't, of course. His head might explode.

I do, however, loop my arm in his, catching him off guard. Something tells me this man isn't often surprised by people, and I'm honored to be among the few.

Dante grows rigid, peering down at me with confusion and shock.

I shine my brightest smile at him and tug him toward the door. "Come on, Mr. Santarossa. The only way out is through."

"That's not true," he counters as I drag him outside. "There are many ways out of a situation without going through it. You look at available resources, possible hurdles, and desired outcomes."

"Mm-hm. Well, it seems you've tried all that when it comes to your father, yet here you are." I give him a pointed look, and I swear to God, he pouts. It's freaking adorable and makes me want to pinch his cheeks. I don't, for fear he might snap my fingers off. "Let's try things my way today."

"Why do I feel like those are famous last words?" he mutters, eyeing me up and down.

I shrug and smile, trying to keep up the positive energy. "I guess we'll find out."

We make it into the house, and I get some water going in the electric kettle for Raul's morning tea and oatmeal. Gathering a mug and bowl, I set them on the counter and pull out a packet of English Breakfast tea, along with the container of steel-cut oats.

Next, I grab the locked box of pills on the counter and dial in the code. One by one, I pull out the various medications. Some for pain, others to regulate the input and output of certain organs, and a few to counteract the side effects of all the other meds.

I notice Dante has barely moved, so I look over my shoulder at him and see him standing in the corner, looking completely out of place. He shuffles his weight from side to side, then crosses his arms before uncrossing them and shoving them in his pockets. Anxiety radiating off him, and I'm sure if I could take a peek behind that steel wall he has around his heart, I'd see it hammering away out of fear.

"That's a lot of pills," Dante says, his words tinged with guilt.

"I've had clients who take more," I say with a shrug. Truthfully, it is a lot because Raul is in bad shape. I seem to be the only one around here not in denial about that. Still, I don't want to pile on when Dante is clearly having a rough day. "Come on," I encourage, waving him over. "You can go ahead and make the coffee."

This earns me another puzzled and slightly offended look from the enigmatic Dante.

I laugh at how shocked he is. "Sorry, but I had to see what you'd do if I gave you an order. You did not disappoint."

Dante furrows his brow, but I'm sure I see the corner of his lip twitch. That's almost a quarter of a smile. I'm determined to get him to show me his full smile one of these days.

"Should my father be drinking coffee with all of that?" He nods toward the cup of pills sitting on the counter.

"The coffee is for you," I say as I pour the boiling water from the kettle into the mug of tea and the bowl of oatmeal. "You clearly need it."

Before Dante can reply, I place everything on a tray and set it on the dining room table in front of Raul's chair as I hear the *click-click-drag* sound of the walker coming down the hall. A moment later, Raul enters the kitchen, giving me as much of a smile as he ever does. Then his gaze falls on Dante, and he scowls.

Good lord, this is going to be a pain in the ass.

"Good morning, Mr. Santarossa!" I say in my most energetic voice. "Dante surprised us by showing up early. Isn't that nice?"

"If you say so," he grumbles.

"Good to see you too," Dante scoffs, turning to face the coffee maker. He busies himself with the task, focusing far too long on measuring out the grounds.

"I didn't ask you to come," Raul mutters.

"Okay!" I exclaim, clapping my hands. "Who's ready for breakfast? Yours is on the table," I tell my client. "And Dante and I will have cereal."

"Excuse me?" Dante chimes in. "Cereal? Like… Raisin Bran?" His nose scrunches up, and the look of horror on his face is priceless. You would've thought I offered him a dirty diaper.

"No, like Fruity Pebbles. I'm not a monster."

Raul chuckles while Dante scowls.

"I'll pass."

"Don't be ungrateful, son," Raul snaps. "Cambria works her ass off around here. If she feeds you cereal, you better take it and thank her."

"I can handle myself, Mr. Santarossa," I interrupt. "Thank you for defending me, but I'll deal with Dante. He can go hungry if he doesn't want my sugary cereal."

This seems to satisfy Raul, and he takes a few bites of oatmeal.

Dante is in the kitchen corner, as far as possible from his father without leaving the room. Raul has his back facing his son, and it's painfully obvious these two have zero social grace, especially when it comes to each other.

"I've got the coffee covered," I tell Dante. "You go sit down at the table."

"Thought you gave me an order, boss," he grunts.

"And now I'm giving you a new one."

Dante opens his mouth to fight me, but I bump him out of the way with my hip. He stares at me, mouth half agape, while I simply wink and shoo him on his way. After a few beats of awkward silence, I roll my eyes and fill up the coffee cups, joining the two stubborn men at the table.

"How was your flight, Dante?" I ask since Raul won't.

"Fine."

I give Raul a look and lightly elbow him. He frowns and moves his arm away from me like a little kid.

"And how is work going for you?" I continue.

"Same as it always is."

Oh my god, this is like pulling teeth. Actually, I'd rather pull teeth. At least that's a pretty straightforward task. Navigating this conversation, however, is a different story.

"Your father recently started–"

Dante's phone rings and he jumps to grab it out of his pocket. Staring at the screen, a look of relief washes over him. "I have to take this," he informs us as he stands from his seat.

"Of course, you do," Raul grunts. "Go ahead. They need you more than I do."

"That's rich coming from a man who depends on me for his home and expensive medical treatments."

"We all know you're not doing it out of love for me," Raul snaps.

"Now, Mr. Santarossa," I butt in.

"That might be the one thing we agree on, old man."

"Dante!" I scold him.

He holds his hands up as he backs away, then turns on his heel and books it out the back door, his phone attached to his ear. I watch him pace around the backyard, then turn back to Raul.

"That went well," he says sarcastically.

"You weren't exactly welcoming," I counter, giving him a pointed look. "Finish up breakfast, and I'll put your shows on. And don't think that because your son is here, I'll let you get out of your daily meditation."

"It's going to take more than *self-reflection* to patch things up with Dante," he sneers.

"Well, why don't you try it first, and if it doesn't work, we'll move on to something more ground-breaking, like starting a conversation or not insulting him in the first thirty seconds of seeing him."

Raul grumbles something, but he's smart enough not to argue with me.

As I sip on my now lukewarm coffee, I wonder if this surprise visit was a terrible idea after all.

CHAPTER FIVE

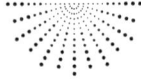

DANTE

"*I* thought Dante was out of town for the week. Why is he calling in for the meeting?" Armando whines.

"I'm gone three days, and you're already looking to take over my position?" I snap.

My eyes wander to the window overlooking the back-yard, immediately settling on the little cottage in the corner. I haven't seen Cambria since lunch, and while that shouldn't bother me, I'm unsettled. What is she doing in there? Meditating? Yoga?

I try not to let myself think about her entertaining a man. For some reason, the thought of her having a boyfriend triggers some long-dormant possessiveness way down deep.

"So be careful, okay?"

I realize I've zoned out the last few moments, and Armando is talking to me.

"You be careful," I shoot back automatically. I don't mean to start shit with him; it just comes naturally.

"Dante," Romeo says, his voice firm and commanding. "Armando is trying to say that the Colombos have noticed your absence. Word on the street is they have their men looking for you."

"Caught a guy going through your garbage," Armando adds. "Took him out with an uppercut and a boot to his neck. You're welcome."

"Really?"

"Are you calling me a liar?" Armando growls.

"No, Jesus," I grunt. "I believe you beat the shit out of someone. I meant I was surprised that someone was at my home, digging through my trash." The meat head snorts. "Thank you for doing your job," I eventually say, my words dripping with sarcasm.

Armando sighs heavily, and I feel a flicker of guilt for a moment. I'm hard on him, and we don't see eye to eye on anything, but he did me a solid.

"I'm not your enemy," Armando says, most of the anger drained from his voice.

"I know," I admit, rubbing a hand down my face. "My head is all fucked up from being here."

"Nah, you've always been an ass."

Romeo and Valentino are also on the line, and both are trying not to laugh. For some reason, I don't mind. I know they're messing around and giving me a hard time, like Cambria. It doesn't sting as much when I think of it that way.

Valentino jumps in and updates us on the latest deal with the UFCW union, which appears to be back to normal. We can launder our money through the union pensions for a small fee. We're still working on getting that fee down, but the money is flowing. For now.

Romeo thanks Valentino for his work, then dismisses him and Armando from his office. It's just him and I now, and I have a feeling the Boss wants to share a few words of wisdom.

"How are things going with your father?" he asks.

I can picture him leaning back in his chair, his hands gripping the armrests as he picks me apart with his dark gaze. Fortunately, he doesn't have the advantage of seeing me in person, but I know he's still going to strike to the heart of the matter.

"About as shitty as I expected," I answer truthfully. I'm drawn to the window again, staring at the little cottage and willing Cambria to walk outside. I need to see her and make sure she's okay.

Silence stretches between us, and I wait for Romeo to finish his assessment of me and my situation. I know he has an opinion and won't be shy about sharing it.

"What's the point of this visit?"

"To see my father."

"Don't be obstinate. If that was it, you've already done it. Why are you still there?"

I let out a breath, my shoulders dropping as I squeeze my eyes shut. "Because the nurse insisted–"

"You don't take orders from nurses," he interjects. "So I'll ask you again. Why are you there?"

I don't correct him, but technically, I took orders from the curvy little nurse that very first morning. She bossed me into making coffee and then bossed me into sitting at the table.

"To… fuck, I don't know. Talk to him, I guess. Make amends and whatever end-of-life bullshit kids are supposed to do with ailing parents."

"Is it that bad?"

I shrug, even though I know he can't see me. Truthfully, I don't want to think about it. I never pictured myself caring about my father's passing. Then again, some part of me always thought we'd have time later.

I finally settle on, "It's not great,"

"And have you talked to your father? Made amends and all that bullshit?" he asks, using my words.

"What do you think?" I grumble.

"I think you're a very private person, which I respect. It's your family and your business, but I think you owe it to yourself to have no regrets, not about this, at least. Say your piece, let him say his, and then you'll know where you stand."

"Yes, Boss."

"Dante, I don't tell you this as your boss. I tell you this as a friend."

I pull my phone away from my ear and stare at it. Sure, Romeo is my closest friend and ally, but we don't talk about it. We certainly don't acknowledge it.

"Thalia has given me a new perspective, or maybe I'm getting a little soft, but you deserve to know your place in my life. And as my friend, I want you to make the most of this visit. It sounds like it may be your last."

Something about that finally breaks through. I don't have more time. "Later" isn't guaranteed. This could be it. Am I okay with leaving things this way forever?

"Thanks," I say after swallowing thickly around the lump in my throat.

We hang up a few minutes later, and I slump against the kitchen counter, rubbing my temples. How do I relate to my old man? How do I have a conversation with him when all I can think about is cleaning up his vomit after he passed out on my tenth birthday? Or collecting his drunk ass from bar after bar when he became belligerent? Or his mottled red and purple face yelling at me and kicking me out at seventeen?

The now familiar sound of my dad shuffling around in his walker echoes down the hall, getting closer and closer by the second. I curse under my breath, then straighten, preparing myself for the battle.

"Just wake up from a nap?" I ask as my father makes his appearance.

"What's it to you?" he snaps, making his way into the kitchen and parking in front of a cupboard.

I take a deep breath, holding back my first response of *fuck you too.*

"Just making conversation," I say instead.

My old man opens the cupboard door and tries grabbing a class, but the walker is in the way, and he can't reach it.

"Here, let me help."

"I got it!" he shouts, shooing me away.

"You clearly don't."

"Bah," he grunts, dismissing me.

He presses himself against the walker and stretches up, but he's still a solid six inches away. Stepping up behind him, I grab the glass and set it on the counter in front of him.

"Coulda done it myself," he mumbles.

"Water?" I ask instead of engaging.

"I can do it myself."

Without arguing, I turn on the faucet and fill the glass, setting it on the counter next to him. "Everything doesn't have to be a fight."

My father glares at me, then begrudgingly takes a sip of water. "You've done enough for me," he finally says, breaking eye contact. "I don't need you getting me drinks, too. I'm already enough of a failure without you rubbing it in."

I blink a few times, not expecting that response. "You're not a failure," I start, though I have nothing to back that up.

He grunts out a bitter laugh. "No? Well then, just a cranky old man dealing with the consequences of a lifetime of bad choices."

We're both quiet for a few moments, letting his words sink in. He's not wrong. "The alcohol was always going to catch up to you," I finally say. "Nothing to do about it now but treat what we can."

I stare out the window, but I can feel my father's eyes on me, studying me for the first time in years. I'd like to say I don't give one goddamn fuck about his opinion, but that'd be a lie. He's my dad. I think some part of me will always want his approval.

"It's not just the alcohol, son. I fucked up with you over and over. I know I did."

Keeping my gaze locked on the little cottage, I try not to listen to his words. I don't want to forgive him, even if I know I should. The front door opens, and out walks Cambria, the sunlight kissing her skin and making her curvy figure glow. White-blonde hair glitters in the waning sunlight, and I get the sudden urge to comb my fingers through it.

"After Diane died, I lost myself. I didn't know how to deal with the grief, and–"

I whip my head around and focus the mounting rage on the man who deserves it the most. "Don't you dare say her fucking name," I spit. "Using her as an excuse for your drinking is despicable. I hoped you'd changed, that maybe facing your mortality would realign your priorities, but I see you're the same excuse-seeking piece of shit I knew you to be all along."

"Dante!" Cambria shouts. I didn't realize she was here. She must have slipped in the back door during my rant.

My breath saws in and out of my lungs as I clench my teeth, never taking my eyes off my pathetic father.

"I lost my best friend," my dad says. "My partner. And you were a kid. I had no idea what to do with you!"

"I lost my mother *and* my father that day," I grit.

"Dante, let's take a break," Cambria says from beside me. She rests her hand on my arm, but I yank it away. "Step away and take a few breaths. You're both saying things you don't mean."

"He means every word," my dad spits out. "He's always resented me. He wishes it were me who died instead of his mother."

"You know what, old man? I–"

"Enough!" Cambria yells. She puts her hand on my chest and shoves me back. I stare at her, then look down at her hand. "Back off. I didn't ask you to come here so you could berate your father. I know things are complicated, and believe me, I know what it's like to grieve, but–"

"You don't know anything," I growl, narrowing my eyes at her. "Not a goddamn thing."

As soon as the words leave my mouth, I wish I could yank them back and swallow them down. Cambria curls in on herself, her bright blue eyes filled with tears, though she doesn't let them fall. Her chin trembles, but it's still held high, like the warrior she is. Jesus, I'm an asshole.

"Cambria…"

Before I can say anything else, she pushes past me and runs out the door. I stare after her, not knowing if I should chase her or give her space.

"She didn't deserve that," my father says flatly.

"I know."

I turn on him, ready to blame him for this as well, but when I finally take my father in, I see he's just as broken as I am.

"I did the same thing her first week here. She got too close to all those feelings I've been trying to drown in booze all these years. I snapped and sent her away in tears. She's not the first nurse I made cry, but she was the first one who stuck around after. She was also the first to stand up to me the next day and demand an apology."

This brings an almost-smile to my lips. I can picture the

little five-foot, curvy woman with her hands on her hips, giving my father a harsh talking-to. "What did you do?"

"I realized the same thing you're about to."

I lift an eyebrow at him, unsure what he's getting at.

"That Cambria is special and worth fighting for."

Another few moments of silent contemplation spread between us, and finally, I know what I have to do.

"Shit," I mutter. "I need to apologize, don't I?"

"Sucks, doesn't it?"

This pulls a chuckle from deep in my chest. We're nowhere near patching things up, but I know my father understands the position I'm in. Maybe there's hope for us after all. We both seem to know Cambria is the key to everything.

Now I need to go make it up to her.

CHAPTER SIX

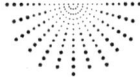

CAMBRIA

As soon as I enter my cottage, I shut the door and collapse against it. The tears I've been holding back rush to the surface, stinging my eyes as they pour out.

After a few deep breaths, I peel myself away from the door and stumble toward the bed, flopping down on it in a pile of pathetic tears. My head is pounding as I try to work through one of my calming exercises, each beat of my heart pulsing painfully in my temples.

Curling up into a ball, I squeeze my eyes shut, attempting to focus on grounding myself instead of berating myself. The old insecurities win out, however, and I replay the entire kitchen scene over and over, feeling like a fool.

What did I think was going to happen? I'd get Dante here for a few days and hope he's willing to bury the hatchet after decades of not talking to his father? Did I expect Raul to flip a switch and suddenly let go of his shame enough to tell his son he loves him?

I sniffle, the unattractive sound making me feel even more like an idiot.

Equally as upsetting is the way Dante snapped.

You don't know anything. Not a goddamn thing.

I must be delusional. I thought Dante and I had some sort of connection, some unspoken bond that had formed over the last few days. Was he annoyed with me the whole time? Am I just a little kid to him? Or maybe I'll never be anything more than the help. I'm good enough to take care of Raul when Dante doesn't want to, but it's not my place to meddle in family affairs.

Some part of me knows it doesn't matter. None of it. Dante will be gone soon, Raul will return to his grumpy ways, and we'll probably never speak of this incident again.

It's for the best.

But then why is my stomach in knots? The thought of never seeing Dante again, of having that be our last interaction, triggers a deep fear. After my mom passed, I promised myself–

My thoughts are cut off by a knock at my door. I tense, not sure I'm ready to face whatever is out there. Am I going to be fired? Is Dante here to yell at me some more? Maybe Raul had a rush of adrenaline from his anger and stormed across the yard to give me a piece of his mind.

"Cambria?"

It's Dante, which isn't surprising. His voice, however, isn't what I expected. Instead of harsh or clipped, he sounds almost... tender.

"I'm sorry. I'm an asshole," he says with a sigh. "I'm sorry for a lot of things in my life, but the way I treated you earlier is at the top of the list."

I sit up in bed, then swing my legs over the side, standing and taking a tentative step toward the door. I hear a muffled thud, and I know Dante is resting his forehead against the scratchy wooden door.

Even though I'm hurt and confused, I can't stand to hear Dante's tortured voice. Closing the distance between us, I

43

turn the knob and open the door, stunned to see the broken man standing before me.

"Jesus," he whispers, his hands automatically coming up to cup my face. "I made you cry." He says it more to himself than to me, and a look of self-loathing and regret fills his face.

Dante wipes my tears away, then gently walks us backward inside the cottage. I'm so stunned and overwhelmed by his tender touch that I don't protest.

"I'm so sorry," Dante says again as he leads me over to the bed. He guides me to sit down, then backs away as if he might hurt me or make me cry again if he's not careful.

He's so broken at this moment, so raw and vulnerable. I've never seen this emotion from him, and I have a feeling he hasn't shown it to anyone in a long time, if ever.

Dante paces in front of me, running his hands through his hair one moment, then shoving them in his pocket the next. He's agitated and angry at himself, flustered that he can't find the words. I watch as he struggles to put his thoughts together, my tears slowly drying the longer I wait.

"My mom," he eventually starts, shaking his head as he tries to get the words out. "She was incredible. This bright, carefree spirit who wanted to bring joy and color to the world around her. Not unlike someone else I know."

He pauses, his brown eyes finding mine. He gives me a tentative smile, and my broken heart starts to mend itself.

"But her light was snuffed out. She was on her way to pick me up from school when she was scraped off the road by an eighteen-wheeler. The driver was over double the legal limit for blood-alcohol levels."

"Oh my god," I murmur, bringing my hand up to cover my mouth. I knew she died when Dante was just a kid, but I didn't know how.

"I was nine," he continues. I get the sense that he needs to get this all out now that he's started. "Imagine my disgust when I found my father passed out with two empty whiskey bottles next to him a few months later. I don't remember him ever touching alcohol before then, but once he had that first drop... I don't know. It took hold of him and never let him go."

Dante shrugs and looks down at his feet. I stand, not realizing I'm moving until I'm right in front of Dante. He lifts his head, those dark eyes latching onto mine and begging me to see his truth.

Resting my hand over his heart, I feel it hammering against my palm. He inhales deeply, then places his hand over mine, the warmth grounding me and tying me to him even more.

"Breathe," I whisper, inhaling deeply as he does the same. I exhale slowly, my eyes never leaving his as we take another deep breath together.

After a moment of silence, Dante continues. "He could have been a workaholic or a hoarder or hell, even done hard drugs, and I would have understood. But poisoning himself with the same shit responsible for my mother's death is extra fucked up."

I nod, validating his experience and hopefully taking on some of his burden.

"The rest of my childhood and teen years consisted of covering for my dad or making excuses for his drinking, dragging him back home when he became too intoxicated to remember where he lived and absorbing his depression and grief while trying to make ends meet. Today, when he used my mother's death as an excuse for his addiction... I lost it. I fucking saw red."

Dante closes his eyes and tilts his head back, his tormented soul on display.

"Breathe," I say softly, pressing my hand against his chest

and feeling his heartbeat. "Inhale for a count of four, and exhale for eight." We take another breath together, surrounded by this fragile moment.

When he opens his eyes again, I don't see any trace of the man who yelled at me. In his place is someone filled with genuine regret. He cut himself open and showed me the raw pain he keeps hidden. That means something to me.

"Anyway, I... I guess I wanted you to know. You deserve to hear the whole story, though none of that excuses the way I treated you. Jesus, I know I screwed up, and I–"

"My mom died when I was eighteen," I blurt.

"I'm so sorry, sunshine," he murmurs as he reaches out to cup the side of my neck.

Hearing his endearment for me fills me with warmth. The whispered, almost reverent way he says it ties my heart closer to his. "I knew she was sick. I thought it was a rare but curable immune disease. That's what she told me," I whisper. Dante doesn't say anything, he just rubs his thumb across my jaw in light, calming strokes. "We went through a lot of different in-home care people as well as a few lengthy stays in the hospital, but I guess I just didn't... I don't know. I didn't want to see all the other warning signs."

Dante furrows his brow, and I shake my head, trying to get on track.

"I'm getting ahead of myself. I was inspired to become a nurse because of my mom's struggles. I was away for my first year of college when... when it happened." Swallowing thickly, I blink back a few tears. "She didn't have a rare immune disease," I whisper. "She had Hodgkin's lymphoma. Some people can live five, ten, or even fifteen years after the initial diagnosis. From what I've pieced together, she was waiting to tell me until I graduated. But..."

I close my eyes and whimper against the flood of emotions welling up, still unable to say it out loud.

46

"But she didn't make it five or ten or fifteen years," Dante finishes for me.

"And I never got a chance to say goodbye," I murmur. I'm not sure he even heard me, but then he freezes. I open my eyes and see that he's completely stricken by my words. "That's why I was so insistent on you coming to visit. I realize now that I just wanted closure for myself. I didn't get to have a last conversation with my parent, but you can. It's not too late."

"Cambria," Dante whispers.

"But I know that was selfish of me. I didn't know the details, and it's none of my business anyway, and-"

"Cambria," he says again, stepping closer as he lets his hands wander down my body. Dante grips my hips and anchors me to him, our bodies pressed together, our hearts beating in time. "You did nothing wrong. You have the purest heart and the sweetest smile, and I'm the monster who made you cry."

"You're not a monster."

"And you're not selfish," he counters. This brings a tiny smile to my face. Dante rests his forehead on mine, his warmth surrounding me and drawing me closer, closer, closer to everything this man is. "Can you forgive me for losing my temper with you? Have I already fucked up everything?"

"I forgive you, Dante," I tell him truthfully, rubbing my nose against his. He gives me a smile, and everything in me clenches and releases. Holy hell, if I thought his scowl was sexy, his smile is on a whole new level.

"Thank God," he murmurs. "If you didn't forgive me, I couldn't do this." He gently tucks a few strands of hair behind my ear, those dark brown eyes filled with vulnerability and unnamed emotions, so different from the man who broke into my cottage a few days ago.

My gaze wanders down the slope of his nose, then rests on his lips, which look soft and welcoming.

"Do what?" I breathe out, swaying closer.

"I'm going to kiss you now, sunshine," he murmurs, his warm breath tickling my skin seconds before his lips claim mine.

Dante teases me with the tip of his tongue, then cups the back of my neck and angles me just right, diving into my mouth with long, passionate strokes. My hands crawl up his torso, slipping under the button-up he's wearing and caressing the dips and curves of his chiseled abs and chest.

"God, your touch…" he groans, his muscles flexing as I run my fingers over them. "You're perfect. So damn perfect."

Dante licks a stripe up my throat, pausing to nip at my pulse point. I let out a surprised squeak, followed by a moan when he sucks on the same spot. My knees tremble when he slides his hands up my body, continuing to leave a trail of kisses up and down my neck. Dante cups my breasts, massaging them and rubbing his thumbs over my tight, sensitive peaks.

"Yes," I whisper desperately, too lost in my pleasure to find my voice.

"You like that, Cambria?" he growls onto my lips, sucking on the bottom one before kissing me properly.

I nod, whimpering into his kiss when he pinches my nipples. Dante hums in approval, nuzzling into the side of my neck as his hand slides down my body and cups my pussy.

I should be embarrassed by how turned on I am, how freaking wet I am for this man, but Dante doesn't mind. It seems to drive him crazy.

This is my first time doing any of this with anyone, but I let my urges take over, chasing the ultimate pleasure I know only Dante can give me. I grind down on his hand, letting him feel all of me.

"Baby, you're killing me," he groans, resting his forehead on mine. "This little pussy is begging to be touched, isn't it?" I nod frantically and wiggle my hips, but Dante just grins. "Need your words."

"I w-want it," I stammer. I barely finish my sentence before Dante backs me into the small kitchen table and lifts me with his hands on my thighs.

I part my legs for him and whimper when he steps in between them and rubs his hard cock over my center.

"Fuck, I feel your heat, baby. Are you wet for me? Do you need this?" He thrusts his hips, hitting my clit through the thin material of my yoga pants and panties.

"Yes, yes, I need you." The words come pouring out of my mouth, almost without my permission.

Dante kisses me again and again, each swipe of his tongue wiping away my fears and doubts until all that's left is his taste, his smell, and his touch.

"Please," I gasp, though I'm not even sure what I'm asking for.

Dante grunts and rubs his fingers against my pussy, over the fabric of my clothes. I grind down on his hand and bury my face in his shoulder to muffle my cries.

"Jesus, you're so damn responsive. I'm hardly even touching you," he grunts.

"So why don't you touch me for real?"

His eyes go dark, and his jaw tenses before he crashes his lips into mine and kisses the breath right out of my lungs. He tears himself away from me, kneeling to press his face into my core, inhaling my scent through the fabric of my clothes.

Dante growls and dips his thumbs into the waistband of my pants. I lift my hips and watch as he peels my yoga pants and panties off in one swift move.

"This okay, Cambria?" he asks, pausing with his hands on my knees, looking me in the eyes to make sure I mean what I say.

I nod. "I want to feel you. I've always wondered what it would be like..." My face burns up at my words, knowing I just gave away my inexperience.

"You've never had anyone taste this juicy cunt, baby?"

His words are so filthy and so...hot. I shake my head no.

"Have you ever had anyone inside of you, Cambria?"

I close my eyes, not wanting to answer his question, and admit just how innocent I am.

"Tell me, sunshine. Tell me I'm the only one. Fucking tell me, Cambria," he demands.

"Only you," I whisper, finally opening my eyes.

"Jesus, you're perfect."

With that, he yanks my legs wide open so I'm spread out before him on the table. Dante flattens his tongue and takes a long, slow lick up the seam of my pussy, stopping to flick my clit and suck on the swollen ball of nerves.

I moan and fall back on the table, allowing Dante to guide one of my legs over his shoulder, followed by the other. I tilt my head and watch as he stares at my pussy. Something about that is inexplicably hot. I clench, and more of my juices leak out of me.

"So wet..." Dante growls before shoving his face between my thighs and making me crazy with need.

He's eating me out in desperate, forceful strokes. His tongue plunges inside my tight little hole, in and out, and then back up to circle my clit. I cry out and claw the table, seeking something to keep me grounded during this hurricane of pleasure.

Dante pulls back for a second, making me whine in frustration. He grabs my hands and puts them on his head. I instantly fist his hair, which causes him to grunt in approval.

"You need to hang on to something, you hang on to *me*."

I nod and shove his head between my legs again, making him chuckle into my soaking-wet folds. I feel the vibrations every-fucking-where, putting me right on the edge.

Dante sucks on my clit and thrusts a finger inside me without warning. I moan at the unexpected invasion and then wiggle my hips to get him to go deeper.

He leans back slightly to watch himself fuck me with his finger. The sloppy wet sounds fill the small room and make me tremble in anticipation. I can't contain the whimper that spills when he adds a second finger. I'm close, so, so close...

Dante's eyes snap to mine. He looks at me like he's going to rip me to shreds with his intense desire. I can't wait to let him. I slam my eyes shut as a delicious wave of ecstasy sweeps through my body and rattles my bones.

"Fuck, that's it, baby," he grunts before leaning down and sucking on my clit in time with the thrusts of his fingers.

I hold my breath as my muscles draw up tight. For a moment, I'm suspended in space, hovering, flying. The hard, merciless rhythm of his tongue is almost painful on my clit, overwhelming in the most glorious way. He twists his fingers and curls them up, breaking the tension over my body as the first wave of my orgasm floods through me.

I bow my back off the table and cry out, my legs slamming shut against his head, trapping him there. Dante slides his hands under my ass and squeezes the soft flesh. Hard. I buck against his mouth as my orgasm drips out of me. The thought of marking him with my release is so filthy and yet such a turn-on. I grind against him again, nearly losing my mind when he growls and bites down on my clit.

The sting of his teeth, followed by his tongue's smooth heat, has aftershocks rippling throughout my body, leaving me breathless and unable to move once I come down.

I'm aware of Dante scooping up my limp body and laying

me down on the bed before crawling in beside me. He guides me to lie across his chest, and I do, snuggling further into his embrace as he wraps me up in his arms.

"Are you okay, sunshine?" he whispers, rubbing calming circles on my back.

"Better than okay," I whisper, my cheeks still flushed from everything we just did.

Dante chuckles, and I prop myself up on his chest, taking in every bit of the sound. "What?" he asks, his eyebrows furrowed adorably.

"Nothing," I say with a smile. "I'm just enjoying your laugh. And smile."

I was trying to be sweet, but Dante's shoulders drop. "You're too good for me," he murmurs, pressing a kiss to my forehead.

"Well, I happen to disagree," I tell him, jutting my chin.

"Is that right?" he says with a smirk, nipping my nose and then my lips.

"Yes. And I want to prove it to you."

Dante stares at me for a few moments, an unreadable expression on his face. Just when I think he's suffering from sudden onset amnesia, Dante blinks and comes back to me.

"I'm ordering pizza tonight," he announces.

I couldn't be more shocked if he told me a saber tooth tiger was outside my window. "I didn't know you ate pizza."

"I'm Italian," he counters, readjusting so he can grab his phone.

I peer over at the screen, then giggle. "That may be true, but I don't think Pizza Barn is winning any authenticity awards."

Dante narrows his eyes at me, and I try suppressing a grin. The next second, he lunges for me, pressing my back against the mattress as he cages me in. "We're having a good old-fashioned movie night. Shitty pizza included."

"At the main house?"

Dante nods, and I cup his cheek, leaning up to give him a quick kiss.

"Thank you," I whisper, blinking back tears. He's trying to connect with his dad. The effort on his part means the world to me.

I'm already falling hard for this man. I just hope he doesn't break my heart when he leaves at the end of the week.

CHAPTER SEVEN

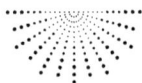

DANTE

I wasn't sure what to expect when I proposed a movie night; I just knew I needed to show Cambria I could do better. I can *be* better— for her.

Looking across the living room at my old man snoring away in his favorite recliner, a sense of peace washes over me. We have a long way to go in mending whatever is left of our relationship, but seeing him at ease settles something deep in my chest.

Hearing Cambria's confession about her mother felt like a punch to the gut. No, that's not accurate. It felt like a searing hot blade being shoved into my chest, cracking it in two. I felt the weight of her guilt with every breath and saw it in every tear that fell from her eyes.

I can't bring her mother back, but I can swallow my pride and try to salvage my relationship with my father. If Cambria found something good in him, maybe there's hope yet. I could say the same for myself. I'm not sure what the bright, sweet, tender-hearted Cambria sees in me, but she found something worth saving.

I just hope she still wants me after discovering what I do

for a living. It never occurred to me to tell her, but now it feels like I'm hiding something.

"What are you thinking about?" Cambria whispers from her spot next to me on the couch.

I peer down at her, smiling at how she's wrapped up in a fuzzy blanket. She has part of it covering her head like a hood, those bright blue eyes shining up at me, and she's so goddamn adorable, I don't know what the fuck to do with myself. I've never had these intense emotions before, never wanted someone so completely, never needed to consume them and make them part of my being.

Jesus, I sound demented.

Instead of admitting all my obsessive thoughts, I rest my arm on the back of the couch, motioning for Cambria to scoot closer. Her cheeks flush pink, which might be my new favorite color. I'm curious how far down that blush goes and what else I can do to bring it out.

"Are you cold, sunshine?" I murmur, sliding a hand into her blanket. Her breath hitches, and she tenses before melting into my side. "I could warm you up."

She nods before I've even finished my sentence, making me smirk.

Carefully, I readjust our positions so Cambria is sitting on my lap, with her back pressed against my chest. She tilts her head back, resting it on my shoulder, and I turn, grazing my lips across her exposed neck.

"That's it, baby," I whisper, covering us with the blanket. "Let me take care of you."

I slide one hand inside her shirt, caressing the soft skin of her stomach as my other hand gently rubs against her core, pressing the fabric of her leggings right up against her heat. She bucks her hips, but I hold her down, soothing her with calming strokes.

"What about Raul?" she asks, suddenly remembering we're not alone.

"You'll just have to be quiet," I tell her, raising an eyebrow in challenge.

She grins and wiggles her ass, making me groan. My dick is hard as a fuckin' fence post, and she's squirming around on my lap in the sweetest torture.

"Shh," she teases, grinding down my thickness.

I grip her hips, freezing her in place while I suck on her neck. "You drive me crazy," I grunt into her skin. Slowly, slowly, I drag a hand from her hip to the waistband of her leggings, flirting with the elastic as she trembles.

"Please," Cambria breathes.

Sliding a finger into her panties, I bite back a growl at how fucking wet she is. Her thighs tighten and snap around my hand, trapping it there. I massage her creamy folds, teasing her and touching her everywhere except where she needs me most.

My woman arches her back, trying to get me to touch her most sensitive spot. "Love how responsive you are," I rasp, circling, circling, circling her clit, feeling it swell but never quite giving in.

Cambria gasps and jerks her hips, and I swear to fucking God, I almost burst. It's like I can feel her excruciating need, her desperate lust, and it only fuels my own.

"Please," she whimpers again, her jagged breaths sawing in and out of her lungs as sweat beads on her forehead.

Unable to hold back any longer, I pinch her clit between my fingers and massage it, holding her down with my other arm across her hips, riding out her pleasure with her.

Right as she's about to hit the point of no return, Raul lets out a huge snore, then snorts himself awake, startling everyone in the room.

Cambria scrambles off me, taking the blanket with her. I

grab the nearest throw pillow and set it on my lap, hoping to hide my massive erection.

"Mr. S-Santa-Santarossa," Cambria stutters, trying to catch her breath. "Is everything all right?"

My father looks confused. His eyes dart from the TV, where the last few minutes of the movie are playing, to me in the corner of the couch and then to Cambria, who's starting to stand.

"Everything is fine," he says, taking a second to clear his throat. "I guess it's time for me to go to bed, eh? Can't keep up with the youths these days."

"Youth?" I ask with a chuckle. "I'm nearly forty."

"And I'm your old man, so don't remind me," he grouses.

Raul's brown eyes glimmer with something close to a smile. I never thought I'd see it again. Never thought I wanted to. But Cambria is changing everything about me.

"I'll bring your meds in," Cambria offers.

"I already set him up with everything in his room," I tell her. "Meds, water, and compression socks. I even turned down the sheets," I say, wagging my eyebrows at her.

She grins, her smile equal parts pride and gratitude. I want her to always look at me like that. I'd do anything to have this woman as mine and for her to be proud of me.

"That's my cue," Raul says as he sits up.

Cambria brings his walker over and helps him stand. He whispers something to her, and she nods, hugging him before sending him to bed.

As soon as my father is out of sight, I tug Cambria into my arms, wrapping them around her as I fuse my lips to hers. She kisses me back with the same intensity, her hands wandering up my chest, desperately clawing at my muscles.

Finally, I step back, chuckling when Cambria sways toward me. "What did he say to you?"

Cambria's lips pull into a soft smile as she looks up at me. "He thanked me for arranging your visit."

"Really?" I wasn't expecting that at all, and I'm not sure what to do with that information.

Cambria nods then takes my hand and laces her fingers through mine. "Want to walk me home?" she asks, her cheeks flushed a deep pink.

"I want to do many things with you tonight, sunshine. If you'll let me." She looks at me with an excited grin, nodding as she tugs me outside.

I storm out the back door, Cambria in tow, ready to claim this woman once and for all. I don't realize I'm sprinting until Cambria pulls on my arm, signaling me to slow down. Instead of changing my pace, I scoop her up and continue running to the little cottage, eager to feast on my woman again.

After shuffling my way inside, I untangle Cambria and set her on the ground, though I don't let her get very far. My hands slide up and down her curves while I kiss her soft, already-swollen lips. She melts against me, her body becoming pliant as I kiss and touch and feel all of her, everything she is.

Cambria runs her hands up my torso and loops her arms around my neck, pulling me back down for a punishing kiss. I open up and take what she's offering, meeting each frantic stroke of her tongue with as much passion and need as she's giving me.

After an hour of teasing and foreplay on the couch, I need this woman more than air. Need every inch of her, need to feel her wrapped around me, moaning my name as I sink deeper and deeper, marking her as mine.

She closes her eyes and tilts her head back, breaking our kiss so she can gulp down air. Her hands drift down to my biceps, where she grips me tightly, keeping me in place. I'm sure as fuck not going anywhere.

I can't keep my lips off her for one goddamn second. I kiss down her neck and lick the hollow of her throat before nipping the sensitive skin there. Cambria moans and digs her nails into my flesh, making me growl and grind my thickness into her heat.

"Gonna lick every inch of your sexy fucking body, Cambria. Then I'm gonna show you how amazing you are. How amazing I can make you feel."

Her eyes pop open, glowing with lust and hunger. Good. I plan to satisfy my woman on every level—carnal, physical, emotional; whatever the fuck she needs, she'll get it from *me* now.

She leans in as I do, our lips crashing together as our need amplifies. Her desperate kiss mirrors my own, her eager hands clawing at my clothes and begging me to give us what we both want. More.

I tear my mouth away from hers long enough to peel her shirt off, and then my lips are back on her skin, trailing down her neck. "Need to be inside you," I murmur into the shell of her ear.

Cambria lets out a sexy, needy whimper as I slip my hand into her tight little yoga pants that have been teasing me all night.

My fingers part her folds and find her clit, massaging circles over the bundle of nerves. "Damn, you need it too, don't you?"

"God, yes, Dante. I need you. Please, please, don't make me wait."

Hearing her beg for me is sweeter than anything I've ever experienced. A wave of pleasure rushes down my spine, drawing my balls up tight and making precum leak out of me like a damn faucet. This woman is my undoing.

I rid her of the last scraps of clothing and lift her into my arms, carrying my incredible woman to bed. I toss her on the mattress and strip down, adrenaline pumping in my veins and urging me to claim her right the fuck now.

Cambria is spread out for me on the bed, her white-blonde hair a tangled mess, her swollen lips slightly parted, her chest heaving with shallow breaths. Goddamn, she's gorgeous. And *mine.* She's all mine.

I climb on the bed and crawl up her body, kissing her thighs, torso, breasts, neck, and finally, her sweet lips. I rub my body against hers, needing that friction, needing to feel her skin against mine.

Cambria captures my lips, her tongue seeking entrance. I give my girl everything she wants, opening my mouth to welcome her kiss. It starts slow, with tentative licks. I groan at her innocence but manage not to take control. Yet.

Cambria explores my mouth, then pulls my bottom lip through her teeth, making me growl. She grins mischievously at me, and fuck, it physically pains me to hold back my orgasm.

"You like knowing you have control over me, sunshine?"

"Mmhm." She nods, her lips twisting into a flirty smile.

Cambria gasps and then giggles as I flip our positions so she's on top. "Then take it, baby. Take control."

She braces herself on my chest, pushing herself up and adjusting to our new position. For a second, Cambria looks unsure of herself, but all of that vanishes when she sees my angry cock trapped between our bodies.

Cambria grabs the fucker and squeezes *hard.* "Jesus Christ," I growl as I clench my fists.

She grins again, knowing exactly the kind of power she has over me. I slide my hands up her thighs and squeeze, helping her rock against me. Cambria licks her damn lips as she rolls her hips, rubbing her pussy up and down my shaft.

The head of my cock taps her clit, and she shivers, repeating the motion.

I cup her tits, weighing them in my hands and brushing my thumbs over her nipples.

"Yes," she hisses, her movements stuttering as she leans into my touch.

I play with her hardened peaks, twisting and plucking them while Cambria claws at my chest and rubs against me, getting herself off without me even entering her. Fuck, it's so damn hot watching her get all worked up, knowing I have so much more in store for her.

Cambria's movements grow frantic as she writhes on top of me. I feel her cream dripping from her pussy, so close to coming already. A shiver runs down her spine, and she holds her breath, preparing for her orgasm. I feel it pushing forward, demanding to be felt, making her whimper with each breath.

Right before it takes her under, I grip her hips and hold her still. Cambria looks down at me with confusion and frustration, but then understanding dawns when I line myself up with her entrance. I groan when I feel her tight little channel pulse around the head of my cock. Goddamn, her greedy little pussy is trying to suck me inside.

"Ready for me, Cambria? Ready to be mine?"

She nods, her hazel eyes glossed over with lust as she circles her hips, trying to get me where she wants me.

I hold her in place above me, not giving in yet. "I need your words, baby. Tell me how much you want this."

"I want you, Dante. I want everything with you. And I want it *now*."

The determined look on her face and the lust crackling between us have me growling like a beast. Cambria eases down the first few inches of my painfully hard shaft, then drops down, swallowing my dick in her tight, wet pussy.

"Jesus, fuck!" I roar, holding her still when she's fully seated. Cambria whimpers, and I lean up to kiss her pain away. "You did so good," I say, trying to make my voice soothing even though the most intense pressure is building inside me, ready to take over and fuck my woman properly. "Take it slow."

She nods and kisses me again, her tense body relaxing as I run my hands up and down her thighs and back. I grip her ass, helping her rock and circle her hips to find what feels good.

"Yes!" Cambria cries out, wiggling her hips and hitting her G-spot against my thick dick. She shudders and moans, rolling her sexy fucking body on top of mine, taking control of her pleasure.

She leans back, resting her hands on my thighs and baring her beautiful body while she rides my cock. I slide one hand up her torso while the other squeezes her ass and opens her up even more for me.

I cup her breast and pinch her nipple, groaning when more of her cream spills out. Jesus, I barely manage to keep it together when I look down and see where we're connected. Watching her soaking wet little cunt stretch obscenely wide to take in my many inches is something I'll remember for the rest of my life.

"That's it, Cambria. That's so fucking it," I growl, moving my hands to her hips, jerking her up and down as I meet her thrust for thrust.

Her pussy flutters around me as her muscles lock up tight. She falls forward, resting her hands on either side of my head. Her lips find mine, and we kiss and fuck like the world is burning down around us, and this is our last chance to find love and passion.

She buries her face into my neck and sobs as her body shakes and tightens around me. My beautiful woman bites my neck and creams all over my cock as she reaches her climax.

Feeling her orgasm devastate her snaps something inside me.

I roll over, changing our position and fucking into that little pussy, unable to control myself. Her back bows off the bed and her legs wrap around me, holding me close. She digs her heels into my ass and claws my back, leaving her mark on me as another orgasm rattles through her.

"So good, baby," I growl, claiming her lips as my own.

I devour her, biting at her lips and spearing my tongue inside her eager mouth, licking up every inch and then sucking on her tongue. It's a wild, messy kiss, one that matches the way I'm fucking her like a goddamn animal.

I slide one hand down her body and grip her ass cheek, changing the angle of her hips and helping her meet me thrust for thrust. My cock scrapes against her most sensitive spot with each fierce stroke.

She's breaking apart for me; I can feel it. Every time I hit the end of her, she cracks a little more, the pressure of her orgasm building and pulsing and pushing her boundaries.

My balls draw up tight as my orgasm gathers in the base of my spine. My rhythm falters slightly as I try to hold on, needing her to come with me. "Get there, baby, fuck, please get there. Need one more from you."

"I don't think I can…"

"I've got you, Cambria. Let go for me. I'm right here. Let go, love. Come for me."

She sucks in a huge breath and holds it, her whole body trembling and then freezing. Every damn muscle is pulled tight as she clings to me with everything she has. With one last brutal thrust, we both shatter.

Cambria floods my cock with her release, and I give her everything in return, my cum splashing into her throbbing pussy as she sucks down every last drop. We grunt, shake, and sweat as we ride that high together.

Eventually, she goes limp in my arms. I bury my face into her neck and pump into her twice more before collapsing. I roll to the side and drape my freshly fucked little angel over my chest.

"Holy shit," she mumbles into my chest, her voice scratchy as she catches her breath.

"Yeah," I agree, as worn out and awed as she is. I mean...fuck. If I didn't know before, I know now. She's it for me. "Are you okay?" Doubt and worry rush in to take the place of euphoria. "I was so rough with–"

Cambria cuts me off with a kiss. "You were perfect," she whispers into my lips before kissing me again. "Absolutely perfect. I can't wait to do it again."

I curse under my breath and tangle my fingers in her hair, angling her head to deepen our kiss. My cock is sore from how hard I fucked her, but damn if he isn't twitching to life, ready for another round.

Cambria automatically curls against me when we break apart, her head resting over my heart. I comb my fingers through her hair, counting the beats of her heart as they slow and settle into an even rhythm.

"You're perfect," I whisper, though I don't think she can hear me.

Soft snores fall from her lips, and I smile, covering us with a blanket before settling down for the greatest night's sleep I've had in a long damn time.

CHAPTER EIGHT

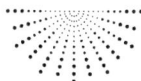

CAMBRIA

I wake to birds chirping outside the window, squinting my eyes against the ray of sunshine peeking through the curtains. Every muscle is deliciously sore, and my entire body flushes with the memory of everything we did last night.

As I slowly become aware of my surroundings. I realize Dante is curled up behind me, his front covering my back in a protective hold. He has one arm tucked under my head as a pillow and the other arm wrapped around my torso, keeping me close.

I carefully turn over in his arms and take in his strong, gorgeous face. I can't help it; I reach out and trace over his thick eyebrows as I watch those long lashes flutter across his cheeks. I let my finger drop down the length of his straight nose before lightly touching the stubble along his jaw.

Dante smiles with his eyes still closed, and I swear I'll remember that look on his face for the rest of my life. His head turns to the side as he kisses my palm. He opens his beautiful brown eyes, and I feel the warmth in them down to my core. I can't help the smile that breaks out on my face.

His hair is messy, his eyelids heavy, yet he looks at me with such… love?

Dante leans in and kisses the tip of my nose, making me giggle.

"You're kind of adorable in the morning," I tell him, tracing his lips.

He opens one eye and quirks up an eyebrow while nipping at my finger.

"Hey!" I giggle again.

"I'm not adorable. I'm handsome." He kisses my forehead. "Manly." He kisses my nose. "And extremely sexy." He takes my lips in a scorching kiss that gets me all kinds of riled up.

"Mmm… and adorable," I smirk.

"Call me adorable one more time, woman," he growls, "And see what happens."

"Adorable," I whisper.

In one swift move, Dante flips me on my back and pins my arms above my head, making me squeal. "What am I?" he asks in mock outrage.

"Adorable," I say again, smiling up at him. I like this playful side.

His lips crash into mine, and he sucks my tongue into his mouth, devouring me before releasing me to let me catch my breath.

"Still think I'm adorable?" he asks, his eyes heated.

I nod, too breathless to give him my words. Dante gives me a devilish grin like he can't wait to prove me wrong. I can't wait, either.

He trails his hands over my shoulders, in between my breasts, over my ribcage and stomach, finally resting on my hips. "Fucking beautiful," he murmurs.

Leaning down again, he kisses me slowly and then blazes a trail of open-mouthed kisses down my neck and over my collarbone. He licks one nipple and pulls it through his teeth, making me whimper.

Dante groans, sending vibrations throughout my entire body. "So perfect, sunshine. Every part of you."

He switches sides and gives my other pebbled peak the same attention. He kisses and nips his way down my body, dipping his tongue into my belly button before scraping his teeth over one hip bone and then the other.

Resting his forehead on my lower abdomen, he buries his nose in my soft mound of curls and takes a deep breath. "My new favorite way to wake up," he grunts, prying my legs open and diving into my core.

"Ohmygod!" I cry out. His tongue feels incredible, warm and wet against my clit.

Dante licks me up and down, dipping his tongue into my entrance and then circling my clit. Again and again. He leans back and looks up at me, my juices glistening on his face. It's unbelievably sexy.

"Delicious," he says before lowering his head and licking me from top to bottom.

He swipes a finger through my slit and gathers some of my wetness, offering me a taste. I automatically suck on his finger, eager to please him. He groans as I circle my tongue around and around before nipping the pad of his finger.

Seemingly satisfied, he turns his attention back to my aching pussy. He focuses on my clit, drawing patterns around my sensitive ball of nerves. And then a finger slides inside me.

"So fucking tight, Cambria. God*damn*."

He thrusts his large finger in and out of me while continuing his assault on my clit. I cry out when he adds a second finger, stretching me in the most deliciously painful way. My legs begin to tremble as the now familiar pressure pools in my belly, and my body starts to give up control.

"Ohmygod, oh, Dante!"

He chuckles into my pussy, sending vibrations all over my body. He doesn't let up, though. It feels like I'm on the brink of exploding. My muscles tense, and I make incoherent noises as his tongue and fingers take me higher, higher, higher until...

"Dante!" I scream. My pussy convulses and gushes as my muscles tense to the point of pain, but in the best, most intense way possible.

"I've got you, baby. Give me one more."

He dips his tongue deep inside my hole, lapping up my release, while his thumb circles my clit. The initial powerful wave of pleasure dies down a bit, but my pussy feels swollen and sensitive as Dante continues to work me up with his skillful mouth.

My second orgasm hits me before I'm prepared for it, the force of ecstasy making me forget to breathe. I cry out and jump when his tongue flicks against my clit.

Dante turns his head and bites the inside of my thigh, then licks away the sting. Crawling up my body, he claims my lips like a starving man. Ironic since he just ate me out and pulled two orgasms from me with his sinful mouth.

I taste myself on him, and it's so fucking hot. His hands are everywhere–pulling my hair, squeezing my breasts, grabbing my hips to pull me closer. I break the kiss to get some much-needed air into my oxygen-deprived lungs. He takes the opportunity to kiss down my neck before resting his head on my shoulder.

"Fuck, sunshine. You come apart so beautifully for me. Love seeing you lose control like that," he says before kissing my neck again. He pulls my earlobe through his teeth, making me moan. "Still think I'm adorable?" he whispers into my ear.

"If I say yes, will you do that again?" I ask, still catching my breath.

Dante chuckles darkly and flips me over on my stomach. I love that he can do whatever he wants with me. Like I'm his. His hands reach under my hips and pull me up so I'm on my hands and knees. Then he leans over, his front covering my back, his hard cock pressing between my ass cheeks.

"I might just spank you, baby," he whispers.

Dante leans back, and I hear a slap before I register the sharp sting on my ass.

"Hey!"

He does it again on the other side. My head falls forward as I try to catch my breath. Why does this feel so fucking *good*? Two fingers plunge into my throbbing core once, twice, three times, and then circle my clit.

Dante pulls his hand away and spanks me four times in a row, alternating sides.

"Dante!" I cry out.

He circles my clit again with one hand as his other hand grabs my hair and twists my head so he can kiss me roughly.

"You like that? My dirty girl likes being spanked?" he whispers against my lips.

Dante doesn't wait for my response before straightening up and smacking my ass again. I feel the sharp sting spike through my blood, setting every nerve ending on fire, which only makes his fingers on my clit feel that much more intense. Dante massages my deliciously sore cheeks. I'm so on edge, he could set me off with a single breath.

As if reading my thoughts, Dante lines up with my entrance and thrusts inside me, hitting me deeper than ever before. I come instantly, crying out his name as my body pulses with pleasure.

He fucks me right through my orgasm, his fingers digging into my hips. "That's it, baby. Let go for me."

He grips my hair again, tugging my head to the side to kiss me while he strokes in and out of my swollen cunt.

Dante sits back up and pulls my cheeks apart, spreading me wide open for him. "Love watching you take my big dick."

He speeds up, fucking me hard and so, so deep. I push back into him, meeting him thrust for thrust. Dante grunts and angles his hips, hitting my most sensitive spot each time he fucks into me.

"Oh god... I'm... I'm going to..."

"Take all of me, baby. Come with my name on your lips."

God, his words are so damn dirty.

Dante spanks me one more time, and I lose control, letting go of everything. Pleasure erupts from my core, rippling outward through every square inch of my body, prickling my skin, and gushing out between my legs. He pistons in and out of me, our skin slapping together, making obscene noises as one orgasm rolls into another.

"Jesus, fuck. So. Damn. Good. *Cambria!*" He roars his release as I shudder out the last of my orgasm.

Dante rolls to the side and wraps me in his arms, my back to his front. We're covered in sweat and panting, but neither of us has the strength to move.

"Is it always that good?" I eventually ask as our breathing slows.

Dante hums and kisses the back of my neck. "I don't remember anyone before you, sunshine," he whispers into the shell of my ear. "But I promise you, it will always be this good for us. You know why?"

I look at him over my shoulder, hanging on his every word. It almost sounds like he's going to profess his love to me, but I know that would be preposterous.

"Why?" I ask, nibbling my bottom lip.

Dante leans in, his lips barely brushing mine when his

phone rings. "Shit," he groans, nipping my lip before rolling over to grab his phone. Frowning at the screen, Dante jumps up and silences the call, then gives me an apologetic look. "I have to take this. It's my boss. Might be a little while."

Though I'm a little disappointed, I nod and give an understanding smile. Dante sees right through me, throwing on his pants and a shirt before kneeling beside me on the bed. His phone rings again, but he silences it. I get the feeling Dante is always on call for work and never lets something go unanswered, so I appreciate his attention and knowing he chose me over answering right away.

"I'll make it up to you later," he murmurs, pressing a kiss to the side of my neck.

"It's not that. I just…" I sigh and look away, but my man isn't having any of that. He cups my chin and draws my face back toward his. "We've slept together twice now, and I don't even know what you do."

Dante's eyes flash with something fierce, but it's gone before I'm even sure what I saw. He dips his head, shielding his face from me as he kisses my cheek. "I'll tell you everything soon," he vows.

"When?"

Dante gives me one last kiss on the nose, then stands up, searching for his shoes. "Tonight. I'll pick up groceries while I'm out and make us my mother's *rigatoni alla carbonara* for dinner at the main house with Raul."

"You cook?"

I never thought I'd see Dante blush, but here he is, cheeks flushed all the way to the tips of his ears. "I haven't had a reason to cook in years, but yes, sunshine. My mother taught me everything she knew before…"

I'm out of bed in the next instant, throwing my arms around him. He catches me and stumbles back a bit, looking down at me with confusion and amusement. "Thank you," I whisper. "Thank you for making an effort. Thank you for showing me more of who you are. Just… thank you."

He gives me that same look from the other day like he can't believe I'm saying these things to him. It hurts my heart, but I'm determined to keep filling his head with positive things until he sees himself the way I see him; worthy of love.

"Never thank me, Cambria. You're the one working your magic. I'm happy to be along for the ride."

I smile and lean in for a kiss, but Dante's phone rings for a third time. He gives me a peck on the lips, then untangles himself from my embrace and answers the phone.

"Yes, Boss, everything is fine. Trouble getting out of bed this morning."

Dante is almost out the door when he turns to me and winks, mouthing the words *totally worth it,* and *I'll see you for dinner* before stepping outside.

I take my time in the shower, lounging in my robe with a cup of tea before getting dressed for the day. It's Saturday, so Raul and I have a more relaxed schedule. During the week, I like to keep him to a routine, but everyone deserves to relax on the weekends. Except for Dante, apparently.

As I make my way up to the main house, I try not to obsess over why he wouldn't tell me what he does for a living. But how hard is it to say *I'm a lawyer* or *I don't have a traditional job? People pay me to take my clothes off so they can stare at my glorious body.*

Okay, so that second one probably isn't the case, but good lord, the man could make a living as a nude model. Not that I want to share him with anyone else. He's all mine and finally trusting me with all the little pieces of his story. I have to be patient while I wait for him to tell me everything.

Raul and I have an easy breakfast of toast and fresh fruit, followed by a few rounds of Connect Four and reruns of

Matlock. It's a pretty typical Saturday, but something feels off.

At first, I think I'm just missing Dante. It's crazy, but the enigmatic man has become essential to my being in the five days he's been here.

While I do wish Dante were here, this is something else. Dante makes me feel on edge, but in a thrilling way. I always feel safe with him, so I'm excited about whatever his dark looks and sinful smirks mean.

This nagging feeling in the back of my mind isn't safe. Not at all. It has the hairs on my neck standing up, making me jump at every slight noise.

Still, I go about my daily chores, picking up clutter here and there, gathering trash bags and replacing the lining, and washing the sheets. The sense of unease grows with each new task, and my stomach is twisted into knots by the time I'm ready to take the garbage out.

"I'll be right back!" I call to Raul as I hoist a trash bag over my shoulder. He doesn't answer, and I assume he's passed out in front of the TV. Nothing puts him to sleep like Matlock, but I learned my lesson not to change the channel, even if he's snoring. Somehow, Raul knows when Andy Griffith isn't on the screen.

I head outside, walking faster than usual to the bins on the other side of the garage. I get a whiff of cigarette smoke, which is odd. According to his medical history, Raul quit smoking a decade ago, and I haven't seen him light up once since I've been here. Plus, it's not like he can hop in a car and buy himself a carton of Marlboros.

By the time I walk back inside, I've convinced myself I'm being paranoid. Probably the lack of sleep last night, with all the times Dante and I gave into our pleasure.

"Ready for lunch?" I ask as soon as I step inside. "How do grilled cheese and tomato soup sound?"

"A little plain for my taste," a raspy voice answers.

I barely have time to register the large man dressed in all black coming toward me before his fingers wrap around my bicep, digging in deep as he grips my arm and drags me into the living room.

"Mr. Santarossa!" I exclaim, trying to break free of the intruder's hold, when I see Raul lying on the ground, his walker tipped over as if they pushed him down.

"Ah-ah, little miss," the man tsks, spinning me around to face him. "So this is the woman who made Dante lose his edge," he says. The man licks his lips and gives me a menacing smile, his yellow teeth and rancid breath making my stomach churn. "A little too big for me, but I guess some people have fetishes."

Rage and terror flood my system, the conflicting emotions tangling in my lungs and making breathing hard.

Who the hell is this guy? Why is he here? What does this have to do with Dante?

"Wh-what are y-you–"

His hand smacks against my cheek before I register the burning pain. My head jerks to the side at the force of his slap, and before I can make a sound, his meaty hand covers my mouth in a punishing hold.

"Shut up, bitch," he snaps, his nearly black eyes narrowing on me. "You're good for one thing; being a bargaining chip."

I dart my gaze from side to side, my breaths growing choppy against the stranger's palm. Something shifts in the corner of my vision, and I hear a roar as Raul drags himself into a standing position and charges the man with his walker, hurling it at him and knocking him off balance.

His grip loosens on my face, and he lets go of my arm to fend off the attack. I spin out of his reach and run to Raul, catching him before he falls again.

"Come on," I hiss, dragging his frail body through the living room. "We have to–"

The front door bursts open, and three more men dressed in all black file inside, stopping us in our tracks. Without a word, one man grabs Raul while another grabs me, forcing us face-down to the ground.

I turn my head to the side, my cheek resting on the carpet as my attacker presses his knee into my back and ties my wrists together. Raul is facing me, his brown eyes filled with anger. He no longer looks like a fragile seventy-five-year-old with a life-threatening disease. No, this Raul is fierce and protective, though his body isn't allowing him to fight back.

"We'll be okay," I tell him, blinking back tears when his arms are yanked backward so they can be tied at the wrists. "Dante will come for us."

"I know," Raul says, nodding as much as he can from that angle. "My son is a good man. He will do what's right."

Those words ease the aches and pains in my body. I never thought I'd hear them from Raul, and I'm terrified he won't get the chance to say them to Dante.

"Aye!" shouts the original intruder, stomping over to us. "Thought I told you to shut the fuck up. Guess I'll have to make you." He kneels in front of me and pulls a syringe out of his pocket.

"No! No, I–"

A needle pricks the side of my neck, and I hear a faint scream, though I'm not sure if it's coming from Raul or me. The world fades, and my vision grows blurry before fizzling out altogether.

Hurry, Dante. We need you...

CHAPTER NINE

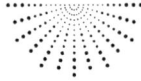

DANTE

*A*fter getting off the phone with Romeo, I took a cab downtown to do some shopping for tonight. Everything has to be perfect. Not just the meal but my words. My actions. I have a chance at happiness, at a future I never knew I wanted. I just need to find the right way to tell Cambria and my father that I'm in the mafia. And convince them to relocate to New York.

No pressure.

As I stroll down Michigan Avenue, I reach into my pocket, my fingers brushing over the little velvet box I purchased from Tiffany & Co. I'm hoping the five-carat diamond ring surrounded by sapphires in a vintage setting will help seal the deal.

Crazy? Obsessive? Over the top? Absolutely. Ask me if I give a single fuck. Cambria is *mine*, and it's time the entire world knows.

I'm about to hail another cab to take me to a market for groceries when my phone buzzes with a text. Probably Romeo with an update on the contract with the meatpacking union, aka the UFCW. Valentino was supposed to settle on a lower fee for their services laundering dirty Di Salvo money earlier today, which is what the call was about this morning.

Looking at the screen, however, I see it's from an unknown number. That's a huge red flag. No one has access to this phone number except those in the inner circle.

I debate what to do for a few moments. If I were in New York, I'd track Romeo down before opening the text. As it is, I'm nearly a thousand miles away with no backup. I didn't think I'd need any for this trip, especially since I only planned to be here for a few days before giving up and flying home.

Another text comes in while I'm making up my mind, this one with an image attachment. I give in and open both texts, my blood pressure spiking when I see what they contain.

I concentrate on not snapping my goddamn phone in half while reading the first text.

Lovely family you have. If you want to see them again, convince Romeo to back off the UFCW.

Unimaginable rage boils up from the depths of my soul when my eyes land on the image attachment. It surges through my veins, pumping adrenaline into every cell and making my muscles scream with the need to pulverize every motherfucker who dared to look at my Cambria, let alone touch her.

My phone shakes as I tighten my grip, my gaze never leaving the screen. Cambria is tied up and slumped against the wall, a piece of Duct tape covering her mouth. Her white-blonde hair is tangled around her face, a mix of dirt and blood woven through the strands. Cambria's head is lolled to the side, her eyes closed. I see a fucking needle mark on her neck, along with bruises, scrapes, and a few open wounds.

Jesus fucking Christ, I can't breathe. My heart comes to a stuttering halt, pain searing through my chest the longer I take in the suffering they put my woman through.

Raul is next to her, his arms also tied behind his back with a piece of tape over his mouth, but it seems they were gentler with him. He's awake, at least, and the rage in his eyes nearly matches mine. I know he doesn't give a shit about himself, but he's ready to murder these men for touching Cambria.

The last thirty years of bitterness and apathy toward my father evaporate instantly, and his words from earlier in the week come back to me.

I realized the same thing you're about to. That Cambria is special and worth fighting for.

"You're goddamn right," I growl, finally tearing my eyes from my phone. The longer I stare at it, the less rational my thoughts are. I've never had a problem focusing my anger into productivity or reining it in enough to come up with a plan, but right now, all I want to do is find those fuckin' Colombos and rip their throats out.

In my hazy rage, I think clearly enough to call Romeo. It goes to voicemail, and I immediately call again. Cursing loudly, I get a few looks from strangers on the sidewalk, but I shoot them a glare that sends them running.

I dial Romeo's office number, hoping desperately that he's there, and left his cell somewhere else. He picks up on the second ring, and I don't let him get a word out before I jump in and tell him the issue.

"They have her. And my father. They... they... they fuckin' got 'em while I was out, tied them up, and, and, and, fuck! Fuck, Romeo, what do I do? Goddamn Colombos have my woman and my dad. They want us to back off the union or else..."

"Dante," comes Armando's voice. Everything in me recoils.

"What the hell—"

"Romeo is, uh, indisposed at the moment."

"Go. Fucking. Get. Him."

"No way, man. If I walked in on him and Thalia, he would pluck my eyes out and chop my dick off before throwing me into the Hudson with a cement brick tied to my neck."

I know he's right, but I don't care. Nothing else matters.

"This is life or death," I grit out.

"Talk to me," Armando says. "I can help."

I scoff, but it's not like I have a choice. "They were digging through my garbage," I say, more to myself than to Armando.

"Yeah, we went over that a few days ago. I didn't know they had tracked you down."

"I didn't either. I didn't think it was a real threat. I just… I wasn't in the right headspace. Fuck, I fucked up, and now they're in danger, and I just found her, and…"

"Calm down, man," Armando interjects.

"Fuck off," I growl.

"I'm serious, Dante. You're no good worked up like this. Trust me. I know you think I'm some idiot who likes to punch things, but I've come a long way since Romeo first found me. It all started with controlling the rage instead of letting it control me. You get what I'm saying?"

"No. I need answers, Armando. I need my hands around their throats. I need to see the life drain from their eyes. I need–"

"To breathe," he finishes for me. "Even if you figure out where they took your father and…"

"Cambria."

"Right. Even if you figure out where they took your father and Cambria, what are you going to do? Barge in by yourself? You'll get them and yourself killed."

I snarl at the thought, but Armando continues.

"And do we know who exactly took her? Was this a

strategic move on the Colombo's part, or did a handful of wannabe's see an opportunity?"

"I don't know. I don't fucking know, but I need to find out."

"Who do we know in Chicago?" Armando asks. "I know you keep up relationships and communications between other families. Never put much stock in that part of your job, but I can see how it's helpful now."

"Right," I breathe out, going through my mental list of contacts in this area. "Chicago is Moscatelli territory."

"Rocco is one of their enforcers," Armando surprises me by adding.

"Yeah, I think that's right. How did you know?"

"Us dumb jocks stick together," he jokes. I don't have it in me to yell at him, and truthfully, I appreciate his level-headedness in this situation. I can't believe I just had that thought about Armando, but this day is fucking with everything I've ever known.

"You get a hold of Rocco, and I'll see if I have Matteo or Luca's number. I have a picture and a number from the kidnappers I'll forward to you."

"I'll get Valentino to run the number and see if we can track it," he offers. "Romeo will be informed of the situation as soon as it's safe to approach him."

I nod, even though I know he can't see me. "Thanks, Armando," I choke, clearing my throat of emotion. Never thought I'd say that, but I don't regret it.

"I've got your back, Dante. We'll find your woman and your father."

A moment after we hang up, an address pops up in the form of a text from Armando. It's an old-school Italian bistro a few blocks away, and I'm sure the Moscatelli family operates it.

Sure enough, as soon as I reach the front door, I'm

ushered inside and led to the back of the restaurant. There, in a separate dining area with dimmed lights and an extravagant bar taking up an entire wall, sit three men in a booth.

"Dante Santarossa," the middle one says, tilting his head toward the light. I can barely make out the strong jawline and furrowed brows in the low lighting, but that voice is one I'd recognize anywhere.

"Matteo Moscatelli," I respond, holding my hand out to shake his.

The man grasps my hand, giving it one good squeeze before dropping it. "I hear you need assistance."

"Yes, I, I mean, my Cambria, uh, well, the nurse who takes care of my father, she…" I clear my throat, trying to get my shit together.

"This is about a woman you love?" Matteo snaps.

I'm not sure if he's about to yell at me, shoot me, or laugh in my face, but I tell him the truth. "Yes. The Colombos followed me here from New York and have my Cambria and my father tied up in a goddamn warehouse somewhere."

Matteo leans forward, resting his elbows on the table as he steeples his hands in front of him. "Why did they follow you here? Are you bringing war to us?"

"No," I'm quick to reply. "The Colombos tried getting in on our territory, taking over one of our businesses. They started this, and they deserve whatever is coming to them. Truthfully, I suspect these fools are acting independently without direct orders from their boss. Either way, they want to use my family as a bargaining chip to scare us away."

"Is it working?"

I growl at the revered mafia boss, who remains stoic as ever. "The Di Salvos will never back down. We are not afraid of anything."

"But you, Dante. Are *you* afraid?"

His dark eyes find mine, and I know we're not high-ranking members from different mafia families at this moment. We're two men who know what it's like to have something precious stolen from them.

Everyone has heard the legend of Matteo and Darlene. When a rival family took Darlene, Matteo went to war for her. It turns out that Darlene was a queen in her own right and handled her shit better than anyone could have imagined.

So, when I answer Matteo, I know I'm talking to a man who understands the stakes.

"I'm fucking terrified to live on a planet where Cambria doesn't exist. I will stop at nothing to bring her back and to keep her safe, with or without your men or your help."

Matteo holds my gaze, his jaw clenched as he assesses me. Finally, with a single nod, I know I have backup.

The back room lights up with a flurry of activity as if everyone was awaiting the signal to spring into action. I suppose they were.

"Did you respond to the text?" Matteo asks.

"Not yet; I didn't know what to do."

"Tell them you'll meet with them to negotiate. I already have my captains searching the area with foot soldiers for any place matching the background of the photo that was sent."

"And we're working on tracing the number of the person who sent you those texts," says the man sitting to the right of Matteo. Luca, his second in command, I assume. We've talked over the phone but never in person.

"Thank you," I say softly, humbled by the work they have already put into place.

I shoot off a text, staring at the screen and willing for a reply with an address. *Give me a goddamn address, and I'll be there.*

Another text comes through at the same time, this one

from Romeo. *Armando filled me in on the situation. The Moscatellis will get you anything you need, and we'll repay them double their efforts. Get your girl and your father and come back to New York.*

I shoot back a text thanking him for his generosity. I should have run this past Romeo before even talking to Matteo, but thankfully, the Boss seems to understand my frantic state of mind. I know he can relate to the safety of the woman he loves being on the line.

"We'll get your family back," Matteo says firmly, bringing me back into the present. His phone rings, and he answers it right away. "Bosco, any news? Southside? Yes. Yes. We'll be there in five."

Guns click and shuffle underneath the table as the men step out of the booth and tuck their pieces away. Matteo lifts the seat of the booth they were just in, revealing a safe. He punches in a code, then opens the top to reveal a stock of weapons.

Luca grabs another gun, along with Matteo. The third man reaches in and then tosses me a pistol. "Just in case," he says. I nod. "Dante, right? Armando told me to watch out for you."

"I don't need a babysitter," I mumble as I check the gun and load the first bullet in the chamber.

He chuckles. "Yeah, he said you'd say that."

I glare at him. "Rocco, I assume?"

"At your service." He holds out his hand, and I take it. "I won't fuck around on this mission," he tells me seriously. "We all know what it's like to have the one person you care about in danger. I promise we'll do everything we can for her."

I swallow past the lump in my throat and nod. "Thank you."

"Let's go, men," Matteo announces.

"Should I wait for them to respond?" I ask.

"If they give us the address, great. If not, we know where they're at. Might as well surprise them."

It makes sense, and I feel foolish for not thinking of it myself. I'm always in control of the situation. I know where everything and everyone is at all times. I've planned for the worst-case and best-case scenarios and have an appropriate weapon for each.

But right now, my mind is flashing hazard lights and shooting daggers into my temples. Fuckin' tension headache won't let up, and I know it won't go away until I have Cambria safe in my arms again.

A handful of minutes later, we pull into what appears to be shipping docks and a crumbling storage facility that have long been abandoned.

"You're sure this is where they're at?" I ask from the back seat. My leg hasn't stopped tapping up and down the entire car ride. I'm crawling out of my skin being cooped up back here.

"One way to find out," Rocco says from beside me.

He reminds me a lot of Armando, and I can see why they would get along. Instead of being annoyed, I find it oddly comforting.

As we climb out of the car, Matteo motions for us to get down. He signals for Luca and Rocco to head around the back of the condemned building, then joins me and points toward the front.

My phone buzzes in my pocket, and I pull it out, showing Matteo a text with the address to the building we're currently standing in front of.

He gives me a satisfied grin, proud of his men for figuring it out. "Perfect timing. They won't be expecting you so soon. Go in, keep them talking, and my men will do the rest. When the bullets start flying, grab your girl. Rocco will get your dad."

I nod, committing the plan to memory. It's not complicated; it's just taking that much mental energy to focus on the next thing. I'm going out of my fucking mind.

"Dante," Matteo grits. His tone is forceful and cannot be ignored. I snap my eyes to his, giving him my full attention. "You can do this. Now, go."

He fades into the shadows around the side of the structure, and I take a deep breath, remembering what Cambria told me all those mornings ago.

It's all about grounding yourself in the moment. Inhale for a count of four, and exhale for eight.

Closing my eyes, I inhale deeply, breathing in her essence, her light, her sunshine, letting everything about my Cambria fill me with purpose. Then I exhale the negativity and bull-shit, focusing on the most important thing in my life. When I open my eyes, I'm ready to burn this fucking building to the ground to get my woman.

I bang on the door and kick it open, not flinching when I'm met with two guns pointing at me. "Where the fuck are they?" I shout, drawing the attention of two other men in the back.

Taking stock of my surroundings, I see four Colombos. With Matteo, Luca, Rocco, and myself, we also have four. I happen to know, however, that Matteo has three dozen men surrounding this building, ready to jump in if necessary.

"Let him in," comes the scratchy voice of one of the men further inside. "Wasn't expecting you so soon."

I squint as I adjust to the much darker lighting in the building. I don't see anything at first, but movement in the corner of the room catches my eye.

"Cambria," I growl, taking a step in her direction.

Her face is swollen where one of these degenerates hit

her. A few blood streaks on her face and clothes hint at other wounds. Jesus, seeing her like this...

She rolls her head to the other side as if it takes every last bit of energy. When she sees me, a heart-shattering whimper falls from her lips. Every muscle tenses, and I'm a coil ready to fucking snap.

"Not so fast," one of the men rasps. "Do we have a deal?"

I stare at him, getting a good look at the stupidest mother fucker to ever walk the planet. He's a few inches over five and a half feet and looks like he's spent his entire life trying to be bigger than he is. I don't recognize him, which only confirms my earlier suspicions. I know all the top-ranking members of the Colombo family, as well as a handful of the Don's favorite Capos. This guy? He's some lackey. Some foot soldier. Some dumb fuck on an ego trip trying to prove himself to his Boss. Pathetic.

"What exactly is your plan here?" I ask the inexperienced thug playing dress up.

The more my eyes adjust to the light, the more I see of his outfit. He's wearing dress slacks, a long trench coat, and a bowler hat. He looks like a goon from the 1940s, and if I weren't two seconds away from blowing his goddamn brains out, I'd laugh at his cartoonish appearance.

"Thought I made that clear," he spits, puffing up his chest.

"Oh, it's clear, all right," I counter, taking a few steps in his direction. All eyes are on me, which is perfect. No one will notice Luca slipping in the back, followed by Rocco. "It's clear you're in way over your head. How many of you are here? Four? Did you convince your BFFs to join you on this suicide mission to impress your Boss?"

"Hey, I–"

"Because that's exactly what this is. Does he even know you're here? Are you working on his behalf, or did you go behind his back and piss off the second in command of the most powerful family in New York fucking City?"

"Well, that's not exactly–"

"From where I'm standing," I continue, towering over him as I draw closer, "this is an amateur job done by kiss-assess who are about to get themselves killed."

"Who do you think you are to come in here like this?" he shouts. "I have all the cards here! I have your girl, your dad, and you have *nothing*."

The short man is shaking, his face a mottled red as he heaves out uneven breaths. I look over his head just in time to catch Matteo's signal. Three shots are fired at once, and I lunge forward, grabbing this fucker's neck and throttling him to the ground before stomping on his ugly as-sin face.

He wails, but I ignore him, leaping over his crumpled body to get to Cambria. Her eyes are filled with tears, and her little nose is red from crying.

"Keep your eyes on me," I tell her as I close the distance between us.

A few more shots are fired, and I see Rocco throw a punch at one of the other men before nodding at me and making his way to my father.

Kneeling in front of my precious woman, I carefully peel the tape off her mouth, cupping her face in one hand and holding her gaze while I cut away the ties around her wrists.

"I'm so sorry, sunshine," I whisper as I tuck a few pieces of her matted hair behind her ear.

Blue eyes sparkle up at me, and *fuck*, I don't deserve the look of gratitude in her eyes. I'm the reason she's roughed up in the first place.

"I knew you'd come for us."

"Always," I vow, pressing a kiss to her forehead. "Now, let's get the fuck out of here."

I scoop Cambria up, thanking every god I can think of

that she's in my arms. She curls up against my chest, and I tuck her head into my shoulder, not wanting her to see any more blood or violence. Never again.

Looking back at my father, he gives me a nod of approval as Rocco helps him up and half-drags him out of the building behind us.

We make it outside, and I run to one of the Moscatelli's vehicles, opening the back door and gently placing Cambria inside. Rocco is close behind me, and he helps my dad into the passenger's seat before hopping into the driver's seat.

I join my woman in the back, pulling her onto my lap and cradling her against me as we wind our way through Chicago.

By the time we pull up to my father's house, Cambria is shaking and nearly hyperventilating. "I've got you, sunshine," I whisper, stroking her cheek. "You're safe now."

She nods, her eyes fluttering closed as she relaxes against me. I can feel the adrenaline leaving her body, and each breath feels like it's draining her of energy.

"I love you, Cambria," I murmur, brushing my lips against hers. "And I'm going to prove it to you somehow."

"You already did," she surprises me by answering. "Now get me inside so I can tell you the same thing without an audience."

My father snorts from the front seat.

Rocco chuckles. "Looks like my job here is done."

I thank him, and we plan to visit before I fly back to New York. Right now, I have more important things on my mind. Like getting my dad tucked into bed, then pampering my woman, and taking care of her every need.

CHAPTER TEN

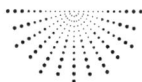

CAMBRIA

"She's resting now, but we'll visit soon. Yes, she's had breakfast. Yes, Dad, I made sure she has plenty of her favorite sleepy-time tea for later. There's no need for you to come over again. You need rest too, old man!"

I can't help the giggle that falls from my lips as I listen to Dante talk to his dad over the phone. They've been suffocating me with attention last night and this morning, ensuring I have water, food, tea, blankets, pillows, and everything else under the sun. I'm not sure who has bossed whom around the most since we got home yesterday, Dante or Raul.

I reminded them that, technically, I was the only person with medical training, but that argument didn't hold any weight. Both men told me to rest and refused to let me help clean up the living room from the intruders or cook dinner. The two of them have been tripping all over themselves to wait on me hand and foot, and it may be the most loved and cherished I've ever felt.

Dante spins around, his brown eyes meeting mine. A

warm sparkle shines from the depths of his soul, and it makes me blush. We still have some things to discuss, like who exactly the Colombos, Moscatellis, and Di Salvos are, but I'm just content to be near my Dante and to have him look at me like this.

"Gotta go, Dad. The patient is up."

I roll my eyes at Dante as he hangs up the phone and strides over to where I'm lying on my little couch. I sit up and pat the spot next to me, smiling when he curls his large frame to fit in the seat.

"How are you feeling after your nap, sunshine?" he asks softly as he cups my chin. "Can I get you anything?" Dante gently turns my head to the left, inspecting a wound on my cheek, then turns it to the right, frowning at a cut on my temple.

"I'm a lot better today," I promise, looping my fingers around his wrist and pulling his hand away from my face. I kiss his fingertips, then nibble on one, making him growl.

"Careful," he warns, those brown eyes flashing dark with lust.

"I don't want to be careful," I say with a pout, scooting closer to Dante. "I just want you," I tell him honestly.

"Cambria, baby, I want you too. Always. But if I hurt you…"

"You won't. You're not capable of it."

"That's where you're wrong," he murmurs, looking away from me. "I'm capable of a lot of horrible things. And I already hurt you by dragging you into my mess. God, Cambria, I'm so fucking sorry. Look what they did to you. Jesus, I'm a monster."

I lean into Dante, placing a hand over his heart. He still refuses to look at me, so I nuzzle into his neck, burrowing ever closer so he knows I'm not going anywhere. "I forgive you, Dante," I whisper. His entire body stills, his muscles growing rigid at my words. "Though not for what you might think. You're not responsible for the actions of others, but you are responsible for telling the truth. So tell me the truth. Who were they? Who are you? What do you do for a living?"

He's quiet for long moments while I hold him, absorbing the doubt and fear radiating off him in waves.

"Whatever it is," I continue softly, "I just want to know who you are. I want to love you. All of you. Please, please let me." Dante's eyes finally meet mine, his brown gaze filled with vulnerability and brokenness. "Don't you know I'll keep you safe too? All the parts you're afraid to show the world, I'll hold them close. I'll protect them."

"Cambria," he murmurs, tilting his head down to rest on mine. "I'm in the mafia," he finally confesses.

My heart thuds against my ribcage as everything clicks into place. That makes sense. The secrecy, the wealth, the demanding schedule, and the Italian family names thrown around like weapons.

"Are you scared of me?" he asks after a beat of silence.

"No," I answer right away. "I trust you, Dante. I trusted you with all of me before I knew, and now that it's out there... I'm just happy we can be honest. That's all I want."

"Maybe you don't understand," Dante protests. "I'm not some foot soldier. I'm the Underboss. The second in command."

He's so serious, and his dark gaze warns me not to push it. But I have to tease him. Just a little. "Brag."

Dante blinks at me, a look of bewilderment on his face. It's priceless. My second favorite look of his. "You really don't care?" he asks slowly.

"I'm proud of you for reaching so close to the top and all, don't get me wrong."

"That's not what I mean." He sighs.

I giggle and readjust on the couch, throwing a leg over his

lap to get properly seated on top of him. Dante's eyes widen, and his hands automatically rest on my hips. I press my forehead against his, needing this closeness.

"I love *you*, Dante. Nothing else matters. Life is complicated, but I know you're a good man. I'd like you to shut up and let me love you forever."

This pulls a chuckle from him, and I smile brightly, enjoying the sound.

"Why are you so good to me, baby?" he murmurs, nibbling down my neck. I tilt my head, giving him better access. "I don't deserve you."

"I can't wait to prove you wrong," I reply before fusing our lips.

I wrap my arms around his neck and hold him close as I grind on his lap. Dante groans and breaks our kiss, only to lick down my neck. I shiver and squeeze my thighs around his hips, needing more.

Dante leans back and cups my face, resting his forehead on mine. We're both breathing heavily, the air thick with what we both crave. He slides his hands down my neck, shoulders, and torso until he grips the hem of my shirt and gently lifts it off my body.

"Are you sure?" he asks, his brown gaze searching mine. "You went through a lot yesterday, and if I hurt you–"

"I love how sweet you are with me," I whisper, cutting him off with a kiss. "And I love that you want to take care of me. Right now, I need to feel you, Dante. Need to be with you like this. Will you give that to me?"

I'm bare before him in more ways than one. I feel vulnerable yet bold. Exposed, yet covered in the safety that is my Dante. My home. My love. His fingertips trail up my sides in featherlight touches as he looks at me with awe and reverence.

"I'll give you anything, love. I need you too."

Leaning forward, Dante captures my nipple in his mouth, gently sucking as his hands slide around to my back, pressing me closer to him. I tip my head back and rock my hips against his, savoring every swipe of his tongue and stroke of his fingers.

Dante hums in approval as he switches breasts, lavishing the other with the same attention. I feel the vibrations deep down in my core, making more of my arousal drip and coat the thin layer of fabric covering his throbbing dick. I feel it swell even more as a soft growl rumbles up from his chest.

I slide my hands down his chiseled chest, pushing him back. He grunts in frustration like I took away his favorite toy. It makes me giggle knowing he wants me that much.

Dante looks up at me with the softest, sweetest smile, making me melt for him even as I'm so turned on that I'm ready to burst.

"Love that sound, sunshine. Love every single time I can get you to laugh."

God, how is this man so freaking perfect? I don't know how to respond to him with words, so I kiss him again as my hands trail lower, lower, lower until my fingers graze the waistband of his boxer briefs.

He tilts his head back, breaking our kiss to growl softly. I scoot back enough to reach inside and pull him out, stroking him and rubbing his precum up and down his thickness.

"Jesus," he grunts, his muscles tensing and flexing as I pick up my pace.

Dante grips my hips and lifts me, positioning me so the head of his cock is right at my entrance. My pussy clenches and releases more of my wetness, helping him to slide in easily.

"This what you need, baby? Need me to fill you up?"

"Yes. God, Dante…" I breathe, moaning as my tight channel stretches to accommodate him.

I feel every vein and ridge of his dick as he enters me. It's so good to be connected like this, to be completed in a way only Dante can provide.

My hands move on their own, tangling in my hair as I stretch my body out for his pleasure. He groans and sucks on my neck as his hands slide up my back and grip my shoulders. He presses my body down on his as he grinds his thick cock against me, hitting my clit just right.

I jerk and tremble in his embrace, gasping for air when he pushes me right to the edge. Dante trails his fingers down my spine, gripping my ass and spreading my cheeks apart as he starts to fuck up into my pulsing cunt.

"Love feeling you, Cambria. Love your sexy fucking body," he murmurs, nipping at my earlobe and causing me to shudder in his arms.

"Mmhm," is all I can manage to say, too lost in the sensation of his cock scraping along my walls and hitting every pleasure point inside of me.

My orgasm blooms deep in my core, throbbing outward and seizing my muscles. My joints lock, and I suck in a breath, bracing myself for what's to come. I squeeze my pussy around him and roll my hips in jerky motions, needing to come so bad it hurts.

Dante senses my urgency, cupping the back of my neck and drawing me down for a heated kiss. He pulls my bottom lip through his teeth before diving in, tangling his tongue with mine as he bounces me off his cock. He tilts his hips and hits that one spot that drives me crazy. Over and over, he hammers into me until the coil snaps, and I cry out my orgasm. Pure pleasure slams into me, overwhelming my senses as I writhe and whimper and get completely swept away by my release.

When I open my eyes, I'm lying on my back, Dante hovering over me and staring at me with a hunger so fierce it makes my cunt contract again, despite my intense orgasm. He growls and begins moving again, his dick still buried deep inside me.

He builds us both up with slow, measured rolls of his hips. His need is palpable, but he's being so gentle with me, sliding in and out, again and again, never breaking eye contact.

Dante cups my face with one hand, wiping away a tear I didn't know was there. He kisses the spot before burying his face into my neck.

"I love you," he murmurs, nuzzling into me as we make love. That's exactly what this is. It's intense, but in a different way than previously. Everything is heightened, our souls tangling together as perfectly as our bodies.

"Dante," I whisper. "I love you so much."

His dick twitches at my words, making me moan. He slides one hand between my back and the couch cushion, pressing me closer to him, needing as much of me as possible. His touch leaves a trail of fire and awareness as he grazes his fingertips over my ass and then grips my thigh. He spreads me open even wider and hooks his hand behind my knee, lifting it and changing the angle.

I gasp and whimper as he hits me so damn deep. My nails dig into his biceps as he slowly pulls out and pushes back in, going deeper with every thrust. Each time he reaches the end of me, I jerk and spasm, electricity flowing through my veins and sparking a fire deep in my core. Flames lick at my nerves as my moans become cries of pleasure, torture, bliss, and an almost painful need for release.

"That's it," he grunts, his hips stuttering as he picks up his pace. "Fuck, I feel you, baby. Are you going to come for me?"

I nod and whimper, my body trembling as I take everything he's giving me. Liquid heat erupts from my core, spilling out of me, making me convulse in his arms as I come around his cock.

Dante grunts and snaps his hips against mine, fucking me roughly as I fall apart. I can't *breathe*. He's so deep, thick, and mind-numbingly incredible. I thought my pleasure had peaked, but I spasm around him again when he unleashes his cum inside me. He grunts his orgasm, grinding his dick down as it jerks and throbs, coating my pussy with his release.

His lips find mine, and he thrusts his tongue inside my mouth, swallowing down my moans and sucking the air out of my lungs. He breaks the kiss, only to scrape his teeth down the side of my neck, across my collarbone, over my breast, and down my torso.

"Wh-what are you…?"

My question is cut off when he settles between my thighs and licks my pussy. I gasp and moan loudly, my body moving on its own to grind against his face. My pussy feels raw and swollen and so damn sensitive from the orgasms I've already had, yet each stroke of his tongue brings me closer, closer, closer to another release.

He growls as he licks up our combined juices. It's so dirty, so fucking filthy. And that only turns me on more. Dante spears his tongue into my entrance, massaging my walls and driving me insane.

My thighs snap around his head when he turns his attention to my clit, sucking on the oversensitized bundle of nerves. I twist in his grip and bow my back off the couch, only to have him spread his hand out over my lower belly and gently press me back down onto the cushions. He keeps his hand there, creating a delicious pressure that radiates from my core.

I claw at the couch as my orgasm fights to the surface, tearing its way out and wringing pleasure from every cell in my body. Dante growls into my pussy, never letting up, using his tongue and teeth expertly to keep me at my peak for so damn long.

I shake and sweat and whimper his name, unable to escape the brutal bliss overwhelming me. An intense, all-consuming pressure tugs at my lower belly. It's unlike anything I've ever experienced, and I'm almost afraid of what's happening to me. My hands tangle in Dante's hair, gripping and twisting the strands, needing him to anchor me here on earth.

Another stronger, wilder orgasm threatens to end me, even as my body reels from my first one. Every muscle draws up tight, my joints locking, my breath frozen in my lungs. Time stands still, waiting, watching as I surrender to the pleasure Dante is bringing me.

All at once, everything inside me unravels. I gush for him, an embarrassing amount of wetness leaving me as I scream and thrash around almost violently.

I can't do anything except whimper and melt, all the strength draining from my body. I'm vaguely aware of Dante scooping me up and carrying me over to the bed, hardly registering when he cleans me up with a damp washcloth.

The bed dips with his weight, though I still can't open my eyes. He drapes my limp body over his, and I automatically curl into his chest. Dante presses a kiss to the top of my head and tucks a blanket around us.

"Sleep now, sunshine," he whispers as he strokes my back in a feather-light touch. "I'll be here when you wake up."

CHAPTER ELEVEN

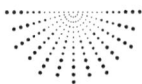

DANTE

I breathe in the warmth and sweetness of my Cambria, her scent lingering on the sheets in the morning light. Today is the day I finally set my plan in motion.

It was supposed to happen several days ago, but the fuckin' Colombos ruined everything. Not this time. I have my woman safe and sound, my father is stable and resting at the main house, the meal is planned and shopped for, and I have a ring burning a hole in my pocket. It's time to claim what's mine.

Rolling over, I'm ready to gather Cambria in my arms and wake her up with a million kisses all over her face, only... she's not here.

I shoot out of bed, hoping my sunshine didn't step out on me. Then I hear the shower running and get all sorts of dirty ideas. Ones that I plan on pursuing very soon.

I'm still naked from the night before, so I walk into the bathroom and marvel at the silhouette of Cambria through the shower curtain. She's so fucking beautiful that it sometimes hurts to look at her.

Pulling the shower curtain back, I'm greeted with the most perfect sight in the world. My woman, dripping wet, with a sexy as fuck grin on her face. I step in and slide my hands all over her body, memorizing every dip and curve before pulling her in for a kiss. God, I missed the taste of her mouth, and it's barely been eight hours.

"I was wondering when you'd join me," she purrs.

I groan into the side of her neck as I suck and nibble her skin the way she likes. She trembles as my mouth works up and down the slender column. Her hand slides down my abs and grips my cock, already hard for her.

"Fuck me," I grunt as I buck my hips into her hand.

She works me over, sliding up and down. "Yeah, that's the idea," she whispers.

I growl and kiss my way down to her perfect breasts, sucking one in my mouth. Cambria inhales sharply and gives me a soft moan that spurs me on as I lick her nipple and scrape my teeth over the hard peak.

I slide a finger up her slit and circle her clit. Cambria's knees shake, and I hold her up, chuckling into her skin. "Love how responsive you are. Are you ready for me?"

"Y-yes, pl-please…oh!" She cries out as I dip a finger into her entrance, still so tight for me.

"You're not too sore?"

"No, ah…I'm ready, oh god, oh my god," her voice cracks as I finger her slowly, building her up and then backing down when she's close to the edge.

Her hand has stopped stroking my dick because she's so caught up in what I'm doing to her. It's probably for the best because I could come just from watching her writhe and melt in my hands, and I want this to last longer.

Cambria grips my biceps and rests her head on my chest, trembling and gasping for air. I love seeing her like this, so lost in lust, in pleasure.

I withdraw my hand, and she whines in protest, giving me the cutest little angry face. I can't help but kiss her as I guide her back to the wall. My hands slide down her curvy frame and grip her ass, lifting her and pinning her to the wall. Her legs automatically go around me, and her arms loop my neck.

Cambria moans so perfectly for me when my cock rubs up and down her slit, the head hitting her clit every time.

"Please, Dante, I can't take any more. Just, please…"

"Please, what, sunshine? Tell me what you want." I thrust harder, faster, growling when her pussy lips try to suck me in. "Tell me what this greedy little cunt needs."

She gets impossibly wetter, her pussy releasing more of her sweet juices as I talk dirty to her. I love that my baby gets off on my filthy words.

"I need… Please… Oh God, fuck me, Dante, fuck me so hard…"

I don't waste another second. I find her entrance and shove my dick inside, hitting her deep and making us both cry out.

"Shit, Cambria." I hold still inside her, relishing how her pussy squeezes me and pulses around my hard shaft.

"You're so big. God, you feel so good." Cambria wriggles in my hands, her body telling me what it needs.

Pulling almost all the way out, I slam back inside, my dick not wanting to be away from his new home any longer than necessary.

"Dante! Yes, oh god…"

Her fingernails dig into my nape as she pulls me down for a heated kiss. Cambria bites my bottom lip as I thrust into her, fucking her good and hard like she asked. I grind my cock deep inside her sweet cunt before pulling out and thrusting back in.

She sucks my tongue inside her mouth and moans

around me, jerking her hips to meet me thrust for thrust. My hands grip her ass tightly, helping her slide up and down my cock.

"Dante, you're so deep like this. So good…"

I grunt in response, unable to say anything else. I'm so lost inside her that words fail me. My spine tingles, my balls draw up tight, and I need her to get there with me.

As if sensing my impending orgasm, Cambria starts shaking, her pussy pulsing, throbbing, begging me to fuck her harder. Our bodies are in perfect sync as I piston in and out. She cries out, a desperate, aching sound escaping her throat. Or maybe that's me. I can't tell anymore.

We grunt, fuck, and kiss with wild abandon. My orgasm rips through me right as her pussy snaps. We come together, scream together, tense and release together. It's intense, primal, and so fucking perfect.

My legs give out as the last of my cum shoots inside her. Gently, I guide us to the shower floor, feeling our combined juices dribble out of Cambria's pussy. It makes me leak more cum inside her, knowing I filled her to the brim. Some part of my brain takes note that we haven't used a condom once, but I can't seem to give a fuck.

Leaning against the shower wall, I hug Cambria into my chest. She buries her head in my neck, her body limp and sated.

"You okay, baby?"

She nods. "So good." It comes out as a sigh, making me smile.

Eventually, I untangle us and help rewash every inch of Cambria before she does the same to me. We dry off and get dressed, and Cambria loops her arm in mine as we walk out of the cottage and up to the main house.

"You okay?" Cambria asks when we get inside. "You're awfully close to brooding."

I chuckle and throw her a wink. "Not brooding," I promise. "Just hoping everything works out this morning."

"Oh? And what do you have planned for this morning, Mr. Santarossa?" she sing-songs as she waltzes in front of me.

I stop her with my hands on her hips, grinning when she lifts on her tip-toes. Her shimmering eyes and radiant warmth make me feel safe, seen, and truly understood for the first time in my life. I planned on doing this differently, but the moment feels right.

I kiss my woman on her pouty lips, cheek, chin, and collarbone before kneeling in front of her. Cambria gasps softly, her hands covering her mouth as she stares down at me.

"I'm planning to make you mine, Mrs. Santarossa," I tell her, my gaze locking on hers as I pull the ring out of my pocket. I gently take her left hand in mine, pulling it away from her mouth to slip on the ring. "I'm planning on making you the happiest, most cherished woman in the world."

"Dante…"

"I love you," I rush to say, needing to get it all out before she can turn me down. "I love you in this terrifying, all-consuming, thrilling way that I'll never get enough of. You're… fuck, sunshine. You're incredible, inside and out, and I need to know you're mine. Forever."

"Are you going to ask me?" she finally squeaks through tears.

"Are you going to say no?" I counter, half joking and half out of my damn mind with nerves. Cambria shakes her head, a smile peeking through her tears. "Cambria, will you–"

"Yes!" she shouts, throwing her arms around me and tackling me to the ground.

I catch her, just like I always will, and wrap myself around her, clinging to the most precious, perfect woman in the world.

"You didn't let me ask," I point out as I brush her hair out of her eyes.

Cambria smiles and leans forward, giving me a peck on the lips. "I got impatient," she says with a shrug. "Plus, I like catching you off guard."

I nip at her lips, making Cambria laugh. "Something tells me you'll be doing plenty of that, my love."

She nods, a mischievous glint in her eyes. Before she can say anything, our moment is uninterrupted by Raul.

"Is everyone decent?" he hollers from the hallway. "I love you kids, but if I see anyone's butt, I'm moving across the country."

Cambria belly laughs while I roll my eyes.

"Mr. Santarossa, did you hear the good news?" Cambria asks excitedly as she jumps up from our position on the floor.

"I did. It seems more appropriate for you to call me dad, doesn't it? None of this Mr. Santarossa bullshit."

My girl beams at the old man, hugging him before helping him sit at the table. I start coffee and water for tea, and Cambria joins me in the kitchen to help with breakfast.

A few minutes later, we're sitting at the table, and I know now is as good a time as any to discuss my plans. Clearing my throat, I fold my napkin and set it down on the table, looking over at my father and Cambria.

"I was thinking," I begin, swallowing thickly. Why is this so difficult? This is what I do. I plan things and execute them. I guess I've never cared about anything the way I do about this. "I could relocate both of you to New York. I'll set you up in whatever situation is best. Cambria and I in one house and Raul in a place next door, or we can shop for a bigger place and have separate wings of the estate. Cambria, you can go back to school, find a new job, or never work again as long as you're happy. And Dad, of course, you'll have the best of the best for healthcare. I know it's a lot to ask, but if you would consider the move–"

"Damn, I owe you twenty bucks," my dad grumbles.

"What?" I ask in confusion. I look over at Cambria, who's grinning from ear to ear. "Is someone going to tell me what's going on?"

My woman stands and walks over to where I'm sitting. I push my chair out, and she plops down on my lap, wrapping her arms around my neck. I'll never get tired of holding her.

"We figured you were going to offer to move us to New York with you. I said you'd buy a mansion and give Raul his own wing. He said there's no way you'd offer to move him in with you."

I stare at her for a few seconds, blinking as I absorb this information. "So, you… want to come with me?"

"Duh," she responds with an eye roll.

I spank her thigh and cup the back of her neck, pulling her down for a punishing kiss. "Still so sassy," I whisper onto her lips.

"Still so fun to sass," she whispers back.

"Okay, okay, kiddos. Enough lovey-dovey shit. Let an old man watch his shows in peace while you go house shopping online."

I chuckle at my father, who's trying to be grumpy, but failing miserably. His brown eyes shine with life, and he can't keep the grin off his face.

Cambria hops off my lap and gets Raul settled in front of the TV while I clear the dishes. When my woman comes skipping back to me, I pull her into my arms and hold her, feeling her soft, curvy body melt into me.

"Go on, lovebirds," my father calls out, waving his hand

above his head to shoo us away. "And try to find me a place with a hot tub. This dump doesn't have one."

I laugh while Cambria gapes at him.

"Come on, love," I whisper into the shell of her ear as I lead her out the back door. "Let's go plan the rest of our lives."

EPILOGUE

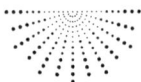

CAMBRIA

"*T*here you guys are!" Thalia shouts, her smile infectious as she skips across the backyard to greet us.

"Auntie T!" our three-year-old, Tanya, exclaims. She lifts her little hands and wiggles her fingers until Thalia scoops her up.

Dante steps up behind me, wrapping his arms around my waist and pulling my back into his front. I sigh and rest my head on his shoulder, loving how he holds me. Whenever we're in the same room, he gravitates toward me, needing to touch me somehow. I don't mind. I love having his hands on me.

"Can I play, Daddy?" Ethan, our five-year-old, asks from beside Dante.

"Go find Cousin Bailey and have her show you her new playground," he suggests, tousling Ethan's messy brown hair.

The energetic toddler makes a revving sound like a race car, and takes off, nearly colliding into Bailey in a fit of giggles.

"Come on and grab some food," Thalia says, carrying

Tanya on her hip. "I'm going to go check on Romeo. He told me he'd be done with work by now." She rolls her eyes, and I nod sympathetically.

"Guess you'll have to remind him who the real boss is," I tease.

"Way ahead of you," she says, wagging her eyebrows.

Dante clears his throat while we laugh, and Thalia spins away to go seduce her man.

"Don't get any ideas about showing me who's boss, sunshine," he whispers into the shell of my ear. His arms tighten around my waist, and I grind against him, giggling when he groans.

"I thought we already established who's boss," I answer, looking at him over my shoulder.

His brown eyes are nearly black, and he narrows his gaze at me, doing nothing to hide his lustful thoughts.

"I seem to remember you following orders from day one, in fact."

Dante pinches my hip, making me squeak. He nuzzles into the side of my neck, sending prickles up and down my spine as his slight stubble scrapes against my skin. He peppers kisses over my soft flesh, then tugs my earlobe through his teeth.

"Love when you sass me, baby," he rasps. "I'm gonna love your punishment even more."

I hold back a moan, reminding myself we're at a family grill out. This man knows how to turn me on with nothing more than a few wandering touches and whispered words.

"This is why I moved out, you know," Raul says from close by. "The public displays of affection were starting to ruin my appetite."

I snap my eyes open, a blush creeping over my cheeks. The old man is frowning, but his eyes shine with pride and love.

"Funny," says Dante. "I thought you moved out because our hot tub didn't have the proper jet system."

Raul chuckles and claps Dante on the back. "You know I'm messing with you, son. I'm grateful for everything you've provided, but mostly, I'm happy to be part of the family."

"Raul," I whisper, resting a hand on his shoulder. "You're going to make me cry."

"And if you make her cry, I'll have to knock you out. Sorry, Pops, those are the rules."

He grins and takes my hand, kissing it before winking. "I better get going then. Wouldn't want to embarrass you in front of your friends."

Dante laughs, and I spin in his arms, wanting to capture his smile. "Thank you," I whisper, kissing him on the cheek.

"For what, sunshine?" he murmurs.

"For loving me. For working through the hard stuff with your dad. For being the best father and most supportive husband. I'm just…" I sniffle, trying to hold back the emotion. Dante's face falls, and even though they are good tears, I know he hates seeing them. "Sorry, I'm so emotional."

"Did I do something? How can I help? What's wrong?"

I place my hand over his heart, stopping him from spiraling. It's one of our favorite calming tools for each other, along with deep breathing and morning meditations. Yes, I *finally* got the brooding, skeptical Dante Santarossa to sit down, shut up, and open himself up to mindfulness.

"Nothing's wrong," I assure my husband. "In fact, I'm hoping it's amazing news." I wasn't sure when I was going to tell Dante, but this feels like the right moment. "I'm such an emotional mess because I found out this morning… we're pregnant."

Dante's eyes widen, and it takes a second for my words to sink in. When they do, his face lights up with a smile, and he lifts me in his arms, spinning me around.

"That's incredible, baby," he croons in between peppering kisses over my face. "Can't wait to get home and show you how excited I am."

I grin and smack his chest playfully. He grabs my hand and kisses each of my fingers.

"I love you, Dante," I breathe.

"I love you so much, Cambria. I never thought I deserved happiness or a family, but these last six years with you have changed everything. I can't wait for what the future holds."

"As long as you're in it, I know it will be incredible."

His lips find mine, and we sway to the pop song playing in the background as we melt into each other. The world fades away until it's just us, sealing our promises with a kiss.

* * *

THE END
Curious about Armando? Get his story here!

Want more mafia goodness?
Check out the Moscatelli Crime Family!

ABOUT THE AUTHOR

Cameron Hart is a USA Today bestselling author of contemporary romance. She writes books with lots of heat, plenty of sweet, and just enough drama to keep things interesting.

Want to meet me? Check out events and book signings I'll be attending across the US: https://www.cameronhart.net/meet-me-in-person/

<u>**Sign up for my newsletter**</u> **and get a free novella!**

🅕 🅞 🅐 🆅🅑 🅖 🅙

ALSO BY CAMERON HART

Check out my other popular series and books!

Mafia, MC, & Bodyguard Romance:

Moscatelli Crime Family Series

Di Salvo Crime Family Series

Chaos MC series

Savage Ride

Ace

Watchdog Protection, Inc.

Mountain Man Romance:

Men of Blackthorne Mountain Series

Bear's Tooth Mountain Men Series

Curvy Girl Romance:

Curvy Temptations Boxset

Infinity

Claiming His Babygirl

Secret Temptations Boxset

At First Sight

Designed by Fate

My Heart & Soul

Finding Her Strength

1012 Curvy Way

Office Romance:

Boss Me Series

Beastly Brute

Executive Rule

Cowboy & Small Town Romance:

Roped in by Love Series

Sequoia Stud Farm

Small Town Love Boxset

Where I Belong

Seducing Sophia

Take Me Home

Forbidden Romance:

Secret Obsession

Secret Protector

Secret Desire

Holiday Romance:

Adored by Landon

Unwrapping His Package

Coming Down Her Chimney

His Christmas Angel

Hungry for Owen

Snow & Her Seven White Lies

Accidental Valentine

For Richer or Poorer

Printed in Dunstable, United Kingdom

67241425R00071